Bound

Merciless Tycoons
Book 2

Via Mari

Cover Design and Interior Design by Silla Webb | Masque of the Red Pen
Published by Book World Ink

To my husband, thank you for always believing in me, supporting my passions, and helping me make all my dreams come true.

Chapter 1

Jenny

WE ARE ESCORTED QUICKLY AND EFFICIENTLY FROM THE LIMO along a path the Carrington security team has managed to clear for us, cordoning the multitude of news and camera crews off to the side of the walk as we enter the New York City Trauma Center.

Brian speaks to the short blonde-haired receptionist sitting behind the expansive curved wood-like counter giving her Kate's parent's names before we are provided with directions to the second floor. The feel of his hand on my back is comforting as we make our way to the elevator.

Just before the doors close Brian taps out a message into his phone. "I'm letting Chase know we're heading up," he says, answering my question before I ask. The elevator doors open just as Chase Prestian walks out of the intensive care unit doors to greet us. He shakes Brian's hand and I go to hug him. "I'm so sorry about Kate's parents, how's she holding up?" I ask, looking into his troubled emerald-colored eyes.

"She has definitely been better. I know she'll be glad to see you. The ICU areas are pretty strict about visitors but as her sister

1

and brother-in-law you're allowed, so follow me," he says, winking at us before entering the trauma unit. The large square nursing station faces patient rooms with blinking monitors that display their vitals overhead. Chase stops briefly, signs us in and the young blonde nurse with blue scrubs glances up to ask our relationship to the Larussios, accepting on faith the concocted relationship and allowing us entry.

My dearest friend in the world is sitting in a chair next to her mother's bedside and as soon as she sees me the tears begin to fall and she rushes into my arms. I hold her tightly against me until her sobs slowly start to subside.

"How's she doing?" I ask, taking in her mom's sleeping form, the multitude of facial lacerations, heavy purple bruising, and all the IVs and machines that surround her.

"They tried to kill my parents with a semi-truck," she says, sobbing against me.

"I know Kate, I'm so sorry," I say, watching the myriad of emotions cross her features.

"She's holding her own. They downgraded her from critical to serious, but I hate that someone did this to her," she says, looking up at me and wiping the tears with the back of her hand.

"How's your dad?" I ask, wishing there was something I could do to ease her pain.

She glances at Chase and he nods at Sheldon who shuts the door before he starts talking. "He's still listed as critical and while we have every reason to believe he's going to pull through, the official word is that he won't. We don't know how far the security team for Carlos was infiltrated and there's a lot at stake related to his business and family that requires immediate attention. Jay's taken over security for both families, and Sheldon's running all ops for Katarina. I was going to ask you before he gets in contact with Scottie if you would mind letting him assist," Chase says.

"We'll help in any way we can. Let him know what you need," Brian says.

"I appreciate that. My dad is with Carlos, why don't we walk over and say hello," Chase says, leading us out of the door and into the hospital room next door.

Brian shakes hands with Don Prestian and the men talk in hushed voices over Carlos Larussio's sleeping frame and the plethora of beeping monitors hooked up to his body while Kate and I catch up. The nurse comes in sometime later to let us know that we'll need to step out for a short time while she tends to Carlos.

"I'm taking Jenny for a bite to eat and then we're going to stop by the office to pick up a few things. We'll be back a little later in the afternoon," Brian says, putting his arm around my waist.

Kate grins at me and I hug my dearest friend close. "I'll tell you all about it very soon," I whisper before Brian and I are escorted down the long hall of the hospital by the security team. Matt is standing guard at the elevator and joins us. As we make our way outside and to the waiting limo, two policeman approach. "Get in the car," Matt says to us, stepping in front of the officers.

"Gentlemen, I hope you understand but with everything that's happened to the Larussio family in the last few days we can't be too cautious. We need to run your badges before allowing you any closer to Mr. Carrington and Ms. Torzial," he says to the officers.

Brian's jaw tightens as Matt talks with the officers and closes the door behind us, but the window is still rolled down a crack and we can hear most of the conversation.

The officers show Matt their badges and he takes pictures of each. "I'm going to have these and your badges verified. In the meantime, what's your business with Mr. Carrington and Ms. Torzial?" Matt asks, texting someone with his cell while the other security members stand guard.

"We are investigating the murder of Ty Channing and need to talk with Jennifer Torzial," the police officer says. I try to absorb what I just heard. Ty is dead and they want to talk with me about it. He'll never come after me again, never rape me again, and I am elated that he's gone, but they must think I did it or know who did. My heart begins to pound, my mouth goes dry and I am finding it difficult to breathe. I feel the band of steel that is Brian's arm pull me closer and tighten around me. "Count with me and inhale deeply each time," he says, starting at ten and working his way back to five until I begin to breathe a little easier.

Brian hits a button in the sleek black limousine and the window rolls all the way down. "She's not talking to anyone without a lawyer. I'll contact my attorney and you can meet us at my condo later in the day," he says to the men talking to Matt and Jay right outside the car.

The officer with dark hair starts to say something, but the taller red-haired officer nods in agreement. "That seems like a reasonable request given the current situation. I'm aware of your relationships with Chase and Katarina Prestian and the recent accident. I apologize for the timing of this. If it makes you feel any better it's simply a routine questioning, but please don't leave town and be sure to call the precinct with a time we can meet before three thirty this afternoon," he says, handing Matt, my personal security detail, a business card before both officers head back to their patrol car.

My breathing is rapid and my heart is pounding. "They want to question me about Ty's murder, they must think I killed him," I say as Brian's strong arms pull me even closer, holding me tightly and kissing the top of my hair.

"Keep breathing, slow breaths, in and out, it will be fine. We both know you didn't do it and if they had anything substantial

4

they would have arrested you or at least took you to the station," he says, softly caressing the side of my cheek with his finger.

I nod, trying to keep my emotions in check. It's no secret I wanted him dead. I've dreamed of it ever since he raped me. "We'll deal with the office tomorrow, let's get you home," he says.

Wes, Brian's driver, navigates the car skillfully through the mid-day city traffic, but as we approach Brian's sky-rise the privacy panel between us and security comes down. "There are paparazzi everywhere. I'll call in backup and have the driver circle around once they're in place," Matt says to Brian.

"Dammit, how did the story break so fast? Get them the fuck out of here," Brian says.

"I can just give them my side of the story so they leave us alone," I say, hating that all of this is happening because of me.

"Sweetheart, I don't want you talking to anyone about this unless you have my attorney by your side and he's expressly given you the okay to speak. Are we clear?" he asks, raising my chin so I have no choice but to meet his eyes as the driver continues down the street past his sky-rise.

I nod and he kisses my lips. "You have nothing to worry about, let me do that," he says, pulling me close and at this very point in time I know that's exactly what I want him to do. I nuzzle into his chest while he begins sending messages on his phone.

"Brian, I hate that I'm so much trouble."

"You're only trouble when you disagree with me, now do as I say and it'll be fine," he says, kissing me again gently on the lips.

"Thank you for helping me. I honestly have no idea how I would deal with this otherwise," I say, scared of the depth of my feelings for him.

"It's not a thing," he says, his eyes lowering to the text he's sending before I can get a closer pulse on his emotions.

It's almost forty minutes later when Matt lets Brian know that we can return to his condo. As we approach, news cameras and crews are still visible, but have been cordoned on either side of the entry way by heavy red ropes and security.

The valet opens Brian's door and he walks around the back of the car to take my hand as security surrounds us and we make our way across the walkway to the entrance of the tallest and most prestigious sky-rise in the city. The smoke-colored glass and steel structure towers above the surrounding buildings in the heart of Manhattan. The uniformed doorman shakes Brian's hand as we enter and head to his private entrance.

Brian keys in the elevator code and we are soon entering his penthouse. Matt is on his phone almost constantly for a short period of time, but then nods to Brian.

"What's going on? I need to know," I say.

"We've managed to avoid the paparazzi, but it seems as though they've taken to fabricating stories without facts," Matt says.

"They're publishing stories about me?" I ask and don't need a verbal confirmation as Brian's hand tightens around my waist.

"Matt, take care of the perimeter and all the security detail. My attorney should be here in the next couple hours. Text me when he arrives," Brian says.

"Will do," Matt says, before he heads downstairs leaving Brian and me alone in the dining room.

"I'm sorry you were dragged into this mess," I say as he takes me into his arms.

"Stop worrying about it and let me deal with it," he says, looking down at me.

"Brian, I don't expect you to fix this. I just appreciate you being here for me," I say. "Then I don't think you've been listening. The only relationship I'm interested in having

is one in which you put your complete trust in me and I take care of your needs. You're mine Sweetheart. I want you to let me take care of you," he says, pulling me into his arms.

I can only nod as his words sink in and I feel all of the tension of the day begin to slowly subside. "Your entire trust in me Sweetheart," he says, wrapping his hand around the back of my neck, pulling me even closer and capturing my lips with his.

"You mean outside of the bedroom?" I ask as he releases me.

"You already know I want control in the bedroom, in life I want to keep you safe, make sure your every need is taken care of and I want you to submit that control to me," he says.

"God, Brian, on one hand it's like a fantasy come true, but my dad's business dreams, my dreams now, I need to make these come true for my family."

"Tell me what you're afraid of," he says, lifting my chin so I have no choice but to look into the storm circulating in those deep crystalline blue eyes.

"Torzial. It's the only way I have of making my dad's dying wish come true. I have to be able to control things in that respect," I say.

"Sweetheart, I love your brilliant mind and the work you do. The only control over Torzial I want is the opportunity to review anything that may be a threat to you or it. I wouldn't do anything less for Carrington Steel," he says.

I nod. "You know in some circles this would make me an extremely weak female," I say, against his lips.

"In the circles that don't matter. In mine, it makes you my perfect match and the woman I want to wake up with every morning," he says against my lips.

I open for him and nip at his lower lip. How is it that he makes every fiber of my being alive and pulsing with need for him?

Chapter 2

Brian

AFTER A FEW LONG MOMENTS I BREAK OUR KISS. "I NEED TO make a few calls before my lawyer arrives, but I want you to be prepared for his intensity. He will drill you, he will need to know every little detail and it will feel like an interrogation, but he's the best fucking defense attorney money can buy. I don't want to leave you alone, but I need to take care of a few things," I say, kissing her on the lips one more time before heading to my study.

I read the messages from my attorney who was on vacation, but following my single text is on his way back to town to take care of this situation. I hit the accept button when my phone buzzes and I see his name show up on the screen. Lawrence Westin Barron III. The best fucking attorney money can buy.

"Can you tell me anything before I get there other than what I'm reading from the blotter and what's splashed all over the news?" Larry asks.

"You already have the police intel?" I ask.

"Brian, you do pay me to know more than you," he says, laughing.

"Fucking A. What do you have?"

"I'm going to be straight with you. It doesn't look good, in fact, looks pretty incriminating at first glance."

"She didn't kill the fucker and even if she did it would have been self-defense, but she didn't."

"You obviously have information that I don't. I'll listen to everything later, but her connections to the Larussio family are, well, let's just say, that in itself adds to the perception of guilt."

"Larry, he fucking attacked her, raped her and then came back to her condo for a redo. He tied her down to her own bed and was going to rape her again, but she shoved her foot into his nose and drove it into his sinus cavity. Too bad she didn't kill the fucker, but she didn't. She just broke his nose. I was there and I was the one that beat the shit out of the asshole, not her."

"Brian, I'm your attorney, I can't listen to this," he says.

"No, you need to fucking hear this. He was alive when he left her apartment and my security team dropped him off at the front entrance of the hospital. I took her home with me after that happened and she's been with me ever since. I understand they removed a piece of bone from his nasal cavity, but he was alive."

"Brian, I didn't know about that, but it's not that simple. He was killed in a very dramatic way and left. I don't yet know all the details, but sounds like it was mafia related and there are emails between her and Dominic Mancini, one of the biggest underbosses in the mafia. The ties between Torzial and the union money laundering scandal don't look good."

"Fuck! I don't have that intel. You need to lay all the details out for me and Scottie. He's in town right now and I'll have him meet with us before you talk with Jenny. Be here before two so we have time to get her comfortable with questions before the police arrive at three," I say before disconnecting.

Fuck me! Dominic Mancini, I knew from Scottie that he

wasn't happy with the Vegas deals Carlos Larussio was planning, but what the hell does he have to do with Torzial Consulting? I hit Scottie's contact and it barely rings before he picks up.

"You know she didn't kill him, make your priority getting her off," I say.

"Our guys are working on it and trying to make a connection. What we know right now is the redesign of the Prestian Corp medical facilities in Chicago included a proposal to use certain companies for the build and manage pharmaceutical costs. The unions and pharm companies are rallying. Katarina Meilers worked for Torzial and was the facilitator for the event in Houston that brought that proposal forward and the quality outcomes began soaring," he says.

"Yeah, I know all that. That's exactly why we hired Torzial to work on the Prestian Corp Medical facilities. We're seeing the same results in Chicago which is why Chase wants to expand nationally," I say.

"You know Ty was given money by the pharm companies and unions in exchange for information about Prestian Corp's pharmaceutical bundling plan. Ty didn't disclose the real intent to create a package that would drive costs down and still allow enough profit margins to continue necessary research and indigent programs or that Prestian Corp intended to use a process that would allow unions to bid on the work of his national expansions. Ty basically used deception to create a burning platform for the pharmaceutical companies and unions to need to know more about what was going on and then charged them for false information," Scottie says.

"Chase was in the process of negotiations with the pharmaceutical companies and my guess is that Ty would have been prosecuted, but instead he was found beaten to within an inch of his life and left with Larussio markings, which anyone knows is a clear indicator that he's the mafia's bitch from there on out. If you're lucky enough to live you're indebted for a lifetime. A day later, Jenny was sent an email from Dominic Mancini asking her to meet with him to discuss union options for the Prestian Corp medical facilities and Las Vegas holdings she is currently working on. I told Larry all this," Scottie says.

"Fuck me. Don't leave me hanging here, what happened next," I say not sure if I really want to hear it, but knowing I need to.

"Well, lad, that's where it all gets a little bit unclear. She replies that she'll meet with him, which puts her right in the middle of a fucking mafia war. Dominic Mancini and Carlos Larussio are tolerant of each other, but make no mistake, nothing good can come out of him contacting Carlos Larussio's daughter's best friend for information about his ventures. As far as the courts are concerned a relationship has been established."

"So that's what you fucking have, a dead body of someone who raped her and would have done it again if we hadn't intervened, and an email from a fucking mafia underboss?"

"Lad, cool off. It's not that simple, he's the most deadly enforcer in the business and they also found her journal," Scottie says.

"How the fuck did they get that without a search warrant and what did it say?" I ask, knowing by the tone of his voice that I'm not going to like his answer.

"I'm looking into it but a lot of detailed descriptions, her dreams of finding him dead, of snuffing the life out of him, and well, castrating him," he says, finally.

"That was in her diary?" I ask, hoping my voice doesn't betray me.

"Yes, lad. Her dream was identical to the way they found him, castrated and with his prized possession hanging out of his mouth," he says.

"Okay, keep me up to speed and tell Larry to find a way to get that fucking journal thrown out as evidence. Have Larry see if Dr. Werther had her write it. If she did, there has to be some sort of patient confidentiality clause we can use," I say.

"Believe me, we're working every angle we've got," he says before hanging up.

I walk into the kitchen and watch her as she fills a tall crystal glass with ice cubes from the refrigerator panel and then hits the water icon until it reaches the top. Her cotton candy colored lips hover around the rim and she takes a few long sips, replenishing and then puts the glass down. She feels me watching her and turns to look at me with those wide green eyes. I can tell she's trying to get her fear and anxiety under control and all I want to do at this very moment is protect her from this crap.

I slide in front of her and take her hands. "My attorney will be here shortly. In the meantime, you have two questions to answer for me," I say, caressing her cheek.

"What are those," she says, sucking a piece of the crushed ice between her teeth.

"Did you kill Ty?" I ask, pushing a strand of her long dark hair away from her eyes.

"I didn't, but I'm really glad that he's gone," she says, looking downward.

"Did you hire someone to kill him?" I ask, knowing this is where things may get a little bit ugly. If I were her, with her connections, I would have had him killed and that's exactly what the prosecutor is going to try to convince the court she did.

"I didn't, but in all honesty, I thought about it. It's what I dreamed about every night," she says.

"I need to ask you one more question. Did your counselor ask you to keep a journal of your feelings about Ty and everything that happened?" I ask.

She gives an affirmative nod and I feel a massive relief that just maybe we can get the fucking journal thrown out as evidence.

"Good, now...last question. What did Dominic Mancini want when you went to meet with him?"

She frowns. "Who is that?" she asks.

She's either lying or she clearly doesn't know. She's been straight up with everything else I've asked. It takes patience and I will myself to remain silent, giving her time to process.

"The name does sound familiar. I received a phone call from someone with a name like that, a voice mail actually. I was asleep and missed the call, didn't recognize it and dialed it back the next morning. No one answered, I hung up, that's all," she says.

"Okay, that's exactly what you're going to tell my lawyer when he gets here," I say.

Larry arrives with Scottie and I introduce him to Jenny. She already knows Scottie. She holds out her hand politely to each man. "Thank you for coming on such short notice," she says to Larry as we make our way to the dining room table and Matt stands by the elevator.

"I'm happy to assist," Larry says, as I pull out a chair for Jenny and he selects the one opposite her and next to Scottie. Celia places a tray with a carafe of coffee, cups, creamer, and sugar on the table before discreetly disappearing. Larry is every bit the professional and begins going over what he knows about Ty Channing and his demise and why he believes she has been sought out for questioning along with what he believes they will ask her.

"Do they think I had anything to do with it?" she asks.

He's not a bullshitter and answers straight from the hip. "If I were a betting man I'd say they believe you hired someone from the mafia to kill the son of a bitch," he says.

She nods, contemplating this. "Yeah, if I were them I would

assume the same thing. Don't think for a minute I didn't want to," she says.

"Let's focus on what really happened," Larry says, going over the strategy and questions he anticipates will be asked and the answers he expects her to use. He's gone through them twice and her responses still sound stilted and awkward. She's looking down, not making eye contact, her cheeks are heated and I can see the anxiety rolling off her from where I sit.

Chapter 3

Jenny

BRIAN'S LAWYER GOES OVER THE QUESTIONS HE THINKS they'll ask me and when I respond he keeps revising my answers. This silver-haired guy with dark glasses intimidates me. I just want the entire thing to be over, but as soon as we finish with one question he wants to run through it again. After close to an hour we're finally done preparing for the police, and Larry spends the next few minutes giving me instruction on allowing time between their questions and my answers. An oblong clock hangs on the dining room wall and I watch the minute hand slowly tick. It feels like hours pass instead of only seconds until finally the officers arrive and Matt escorts them from the elevator.

I hear him talking before he shows them into the dining room. The taller one with reddish hair looks around at his surroundings before taking a seat, but the shorter, darker-haired man is all business, selecting a chair directly across from me, pulling a pen and pad out of his coat pocket.

His eyes are intense. Little beady black things that make my skin crawl. His questioning style is fast and direct and I've barely answered one question before he's asking me another. He's only on his fourth question.

"Can you tell us what your relationship with Ty was?" he asks, his eyes settling on my chest as he waits for my answer. He's undressing me while he's accusing me of killing the person that raped me. He doesn't know it yet, but I'm seriously going to lose it.

"My eyes are up here, asshole," I say. Brian's jaw tightens as he takes in the officer's eyes' quick shift from my chest to my face. His lawyer starts to say something, but is cut off by the taller officer.

"Ma'am, I'll try to make this as easy as possible, but we need to establish your relationship with the victim and determine where you were the night of the murder. The next few questions may be uncomfortable, but please know it's simply policy," he says.

I nod. "Go ahead. I'll try to answer them and let's hope your partner can keep his focus on the job," I say.

"Yes, ma'am," he says and I don't even glance at the other officer to see if he's embarrassed or remorseful because I can feel the intensity of his anger.

The redhead walks me through a few basic questions, establishing my relationship, the duration of it, and the last time I saw him alive. "Good, ready to move on to a few slightly more uncomfortable questions?" the officer asks.

A part of me wishes desperately for it just to be over. I know Matt will escort them out at my request, but I also realize that it will do absolutely nothing but land me at the police station to answer the same questions another day. "No problem, let's continue," I say.

I do not answer any question right away, just like we've rehearsed. I need to give Larry, Brian's lawyer, time to object if he's going to without raising suspicion. Every once in a while he intervenes and the police officers ask questions in a different way. I've been well prepared and I'm aware that we've now moved into good cop, bad cop since the beady-eyed asshole is now intermittently drilling me with questions.

"How often did you and the deceased have restrained sexual activities?" he asks.

I think my heart has literally stopped. At first I don't think I heard him correctly, but as the initial shock wears off I know I did. Brian's jaw is clenched tightly, but I see his lawyer's eyes and he hasn't objected to the question. He's going to allow it and wants me to answer it. It gets very close to the same question that I feared would be asked if I had charged Ty with raping me.

Would they learn I fantasized about being restrained and throw the allegations out simply because I thought about sex in this way? I know the attorney suggested that I come clean and share the rape, but the beady little eyes are watching me. The pulse in his neck is throbbing while he waits for me to answer. Fucking pervert!

"I'm happy to answer your question, but absolutely not when we're in the room with your partner. He's literally undressed me with his eyes while questioning me and you can see for yourself that his face is red and his pulse is throbbing. The conversation is turning him on and it's disgusting to me. Matt, please see him out," I say.

Matt's jaw is locked and he's already standing by the officer's side as he gets up from his chair. "I don't know who you think you are Miss High and Mighty, but we're doing you a favor coming here. If I leave we'll haul your ass down to the precinct for questioning, which we should have done to begin with," the beady one says.

Brian comes out of his seat, but his lawyer restrains him by placing a hand on his forearm. "I'll take care of this. Officer Ryan, we're happy for you to stay and continue whatever questioning is necessary, but my client will not be subjected to harassment by your partner. We've all witnessed the overtures here. I will contact the judge personally if we need to hold questioning in a different venue as a result of the obvious sexual innuendos and gawking that has occurred here today. Completely unbecoming of an officer in the profession," he says, sliding his glasses past the bridge of his nose. If I thought he was intimidating before it's nothing compared to this.

The small dark-haired man glares at me. "We did you a solid by coming here and you're going to treat me that way?" he says and Matt already has his hand on his shoulder.

"Get him the fuck out, Matt," Brian says quietly.

"Excuse us for a moment," Officer Ryan says as he walks his partner toward the elevator.

"Restrain yourself," Larry says to Brian and I realize it's the first time I've ever heard anyone tell Brian Carrington what to do.

After a few moments of conversation the red-haired officer returns. "As you can imagine, my partner and I have many ongoing investigations. In the interest of easing the situation and allowing us to continue to progress in the others, Officer Rourke has graciously agreed to let me continue the questioning alone," he says.

Matt needed no further prompting and has already pushed him into the elevator and is on his way back to the table.

The officer starts in again, asking me questions; my whereabouts the night of the murder, my connection with Kate and her family and why Ty and I broke up, but he doesn't go back to his partner's original question about restrained sexual activities. I make a mental note to ask Larry why he allowed it later.

"According to our records you spent a few months staying at Ty's apartment more often than not. Can you tell me why you broke up?" he asks.

"Yes, irreconcilable differences."

"Would you care to elaborate?" he asks.

"No."

"Ma'am, I'm just trying to solve a murder," he says.

"You might want to start by interrogating the right people."

"The evening you left Ty's in a taxicab was the last night you were seen coming into or out of his apartment. Is that correct?" he asks.

"Yes, it was the day we broke up," I say, cringing internally at the memory.

"We spoke with the taxicab driver and know that when you got into the car your lip had been split open and was still bleeding. Do you want to tell me anything about that?" he asks.

"No, I think you'll make your own assumptions either way," I say, the response coming out easily after the prep session with Brian's attorney.

"Ma'am, I know these questions are difficult, but we are trying to get to the bottom of this. I know you'd like to have this over with and in the past, too," he says.

"Agreed. I'm sorry, please continue," I say and internally applaud my newly found acting skills.

"Do you know anything about Ty Channing's work with the pharmaceutical companies and unions?" he asks and I pause, as if contemplating my response.

"I believe Ms. Torzial has already answered your question around this topic. If we are going to start asking the same questions over again, just in a different manner then I think this session has come to an end," Larry intervenes.

"Understood, sir," the officer says, extending his hand to first Larry and then to Brian before shaking my own and following Matt to the elevator.

Chapter 4

Brian

AN HOUR AND A HALF LATER SHE HAS ANSWERED EVERY ONE OF his questions exactly as we've discussed. I'm impressed with her resilience, but after it's clear he doesn't have anything new to ask I've had enough and fortunately for the police officer, Larry intervenes and lets him know the meeting's over.

"We sincerely hope you find that bastard's killer so we can congratulate him," I say, as the officer enters the elevator, winning me a scowl by Scottie and my lawyer and a wide grin from Matt.

The police officer actually smiles at me. "We hope to find the guilty party as quickly as possible and put all of this behind us. I appreciate you taking the time to talk with me and I'll let you know if I have any more questions," he says.

"Thanks for everything," I say to Larry, shaking his hand after the officer has left.

"You're welcome. I'll connect with Judge Cartwright and let him know what transpired, but in the meantime, I need more to go on," he says, glancing Scottie's way.

"We're working on it from every angle and I've already asked the crew to begin running a profile on the beady eyed fucker. It's going to be an all-nighter. Maybe you could have Celia have some coffee and scones sent up for me and the lads," he says before he and Larry enter the elevator to leave.

As soon as the doors close and we're alone Jenny's mask falls and she turns making a beeline for the bedroom. I let her go and take a moment to send a message to Scottie.

Message: No mention of the email that the police have in evidence. Find out more. Whoever has the fucking email hasn't turned it in and has to be dirty.

I open the door to the bedroom and she's lying face down on the bed. I slide in next to her and flip her so she's facing me. "What's on your mind, Sweetheart" I say, kissing and nipping her bottom lip.

"I told the truth, Brian. I didn't kill him, but if I were the jury, I would convict me."

"I don't want you to worry about things you can't control. That's my job now," I say, closing off any discussion and argument for a few moments by capturing her lips.

She squirms underneath me. "I know Brian, but they think I'm guilty and the police know that I had a split lip and even about the restrained sex," she says.

I know where her thoughts are going. "No, what he was asking you is if you and Ty had restrained consensual sex. He didn't ask if Ty tied you up and raped you. What I want Scottie to find out is why he asked about restrained sex to begin with, how the police knew to ask that."

"Is that why Larry allowed the question?" she asks.

"Exactly, he wanted to see where it was going to go, what other information they may have that would help us with the case."

"I'm sorry. I should have just answered the question. I didn't know," she says, looking up at me with those big green eyes and all I want to do is make this shit go away for her.

"We can get the information differently, but no one is ever going to know the truth unless you tell them," I say, caressing her soft creamy cheek with my finger.

"I know, I'm just not ready, Brian. I can't do it, maybe at some point, but not right now."

"That's something that you have to come to terms with in time, Sweetheart. I'm not going to push you on this, but by not telling them you do leave yourself open to their interpretations and what I don't want to happen is for you to end up getting caught in a lie trying to circumvent the truth. That would discredit you to the jury if it ever comes to that," he says.

"You think I'm going to be arrested?" she says, her wide green eyes scanning my own.

Fuck, I can't lie to her. "We all know it's bullshit, but we're not sure if they have enough information to warrant charging you," I say, and cringe at the emotions swirling in her eyes.

She nods, contemplating what I've said. "It's been a long day. I just want to forget about everything that happened today," she says.

I pull her into my arms and kiss her mouth and my dick twitches at the softness of her lips and lustful look in her hazy green eyes. I undress her and in one swift move flip her over, tying her hands to the hooks that are carved discreetly into the wrought iron design of the headboard. I fucking love that she trusts me to give her this escape.

Her head lays flush on the mattress and I move her knees forward causing her ass to thrust into the air, completely on display for me. "I'll make you forget everything except what your body wants and loves, but first I'm going to punish you for deviating from the script today," I say, smacking her ass cheek hard with my hand, hearing her moan as she pushes back against me.

My cock jerks its approval. "Is that what you wanted Sweetheart?" I ask as my hand lands the second and third time, starting to turn her bottom a nice rosy color.

"Yes," she says, barely a whisper, but her body shamelessly arches towards the rigid hardness of my cock pulsing between her heated cheeks and that's the only response I need.

"When you raise that little ass up in the air for me like that all I can think about is sinking my cock balls deep inside of it," I say.

A soft moan escapes her. "That's what I want," she says as I rub her little bud.

My cock twitches at the thought, but it is way too soon. "This takes proper training and I want to be gentle with you," I say, my finger skimming over the delicate area.

She nods and without another word I flip her back over in her restraints and capture her candy colored lips, and the sweetness inside. I nuzzle her ears, then her neck and suck so hard in the sensitive area between her collarbone that I know she'll have marks. She starts to purr for me and I make my way to her creamy breasts and let my tongue wash over the erect nubs, teasing them before nipping them with my teeth. She cries out and softly moans and I slip a finger inside of her to feel the wetness between her legs.

I unbuckle and slide the condom over my engorged length before pushing the restraining fabric down so I can feel her, grasping her hips, lifting her into the air. "Wrap your legs around my waist," I command, pushing against her. She is wet and slick, allowing me to glide into her in one easy stroke.

"Oh, my God, Brian," she moans as I push into her deep, causing me to lose more of my pre-cum inside of her.

"Slow Sweetheart, if you come, I will spank you," I say, knowing she's on the edge and will have to fight hard to hold back.

"I can't last any longer," she pants, grasping around my neck, her ankles locked together behind my back, pulling me in as deep as possible while I thrust against that special spot.

Her pussy is clenching around me and her thighs are trembling. She is almost there and she's desperately trying to control the waves that are building, but she can't and cries out as I feel the tremors overtake her.

The feel of her shaking uncontrollably on the end of my dick is almost too much to take, but I want this to last and I told her not to come.

"Oh, Sweetheart, you're going to pay for that," I say, watching her intently as I raise first one leg and then the other, placing them over my shoulders.

"How does that make you feel?" I ask.

"Hmm, spread out, on display and so good," she moans as I slowly penetrate her, driving in deep and then pulling out slowly so the head of my erection is barely inside of her, and then gradually sinking in again.

She mewls, grasping the sheets with her hands. "That's the spot isn't it," I say, knowing she's tilted in just the right position and I don't stop hitting that button, slow but hard, pulling in and then out. She's panting and calling my name and when the waves hit again, hard and fast, I drive into her deeper causing the orgasm ripping through her to go on and on before allowing my own incredible release.

I roll her over still connected and reach up to release her from her restraints. Her arms settle around my neck and her lips find mine. I hold her for a long time, losing myself in the way her body feels pressed against me and the soft gentle sounds of her breathing. I kiss the top of her hair as her eyes close and she drifts to sleep. I watch her and the desire to protect her is almost primal. I know she didn't kill that fucker, but she had every right to. I keep her in my arms for a short while before reluctantly pulling out. I can't sit idly by. I send a note to Scottie.

Message: Anything yet?

Reply: Let's get on the secure line. Give me ten minutes.

I disentangle myself and pull the comforter over her before cleaning up and heading into my study, closing the door, and settling into my black leather swivel chair. I glance at the clock. Still one minute to go. Fuck it! I can't wait and hit the button that will connect me to Scottie. He picks up on the first ring. "What did you find out?" I say.

"We're pretty certain that Carlos's brother initiated the assault on Ty that landed him in the hospital with the Larussio markings. If they had wanted him dead they would have killed him, but they didn't. They wanted him beat within an inch of his life and it to lead the police to the Larussio family. It worked, the police suspected Carlos right away."

"Then can you explain why the fuck they're looking at Jenny for this? I say, not divulging that I already know.

"Lad, think about it. His body is found with his member hanging out of his mouth— a clear mafia sign. The police do an investigation and learn she's been his partner and all of a sudden she moves out of his apartment and a couple days later he's in the hospital with Larussio markings. The officers investigate and learn the cabbie who picked Jenny up and took her back to her apartment documented that she had a split lip, blood running down her chin and was sobbing. She's got connections to the mafia through her best friend and voila, a case is made," Scottie says.

"Fuck, and now they like Jenny for this murder? The police didn't say a fucking word about the email they have," I say.

"I caught that. Whoever did it wanted the body to be found

just like it was, otherwise they would have weighted it and tossed it in the lake. The PD probably just wants to get the case closed fast.

"So not the mafia?" I say.

"Wish it were that easy. Word on the street is there isn't much love lost between Mancini's crew and the old world family. There are more pieces to this puzzle than meet the eye my friend. We're still trying to put it together, but it doesn't help the case that she's not coming clean about the email and the police haven't mentioned it," Scottie says.

"Figure it out. She can't go down for this," I say, knowing he's right and that I've thought the same thing.

"We've got everyone of our intel on the job and have partnered with Prestian's group. Jay's been very accommodating. He's pretty much given me free reign with one of his teams since he's working on trying to find out who put the hit out on Carlos and his wife. Sounds like the head of Larussio's security got turned, probably loyal to Tony and the Italian side of the family and not Carlos is the word on the street," Scottie says.

"Do what you need to do to prove her innocence," I say.

"We'll get it figured out, but I'm going to have Matt stay a little closer to Jenny than he's been in the past couple days."

"Why?"

"I want him with you both in case we need to get you into the safe room or up in the air on a moment's notice," he says.

I can't argue. As much as the thought of someone else besides me taking care of her pisses me off, her safety is a priority. "Do what you need to do, but keep me up to date," I say.

Chapter 5

Jenny

I WAKE TO THE SOUND OF KATE'S RINGTONE AND immediately hit the accept button. "Hi there. How are your parents?" I ask.

"They're getting better every hour, but I need someone to talk to. Chase has been on a call with intel forever and Mom's been sleeping quite a bit," she says.

"How's your dad, Kate?" I ask.

There's a brief pause and I hear her swallow. "The swelling is down, but they won't really know any more until he comes out of the coma. If everything goes as planned they'll start decreasing his meds after the doctor rounds this morning," she says.

"Did they say how long it would take for him to wake up?" I ask.

"The nurse told me every situation is different, it could be hours or days," she says barely above a whisper.

My heart aches for my friend. "Hang in there, Kate. He has a lot to live for. Brian and I were planning to stop by later in the day yesterday, but a few things came up. We'll try to get there soon," I say, keeping the investigation to myself. She has enough to worry about right now without knowing I'm being questioned.

"That sounds good. Brian called Chase yesterday and let him know that you would be here today. In the meantime, I think I'll get caught up on email until the doctor arrives."

"Okay, but don't worry about the Torzial work. You've got enough on your plate and I'm feeling a lot better," I say.

"I'm so glad to hear that. I worry about you," Kate says.

"I know you do, but there's no need. I'll see you soon," I say before disconnecting and heading into the bathroom to get ready for the day.

I find Brian at the table scowling at the Mac screen in front of him. "I thought after last night you would have a smile on your face," I tease.

He looks up. "Glad to see you're feeling so sassy."

"Better than that, I'm feeling really good. Must be all the sex," I say, pouring myself a cup of coffee before sitting beside him.

"Always glad to be of service," he says, smirking.

"I talked to Kate. She said they're going to start the process for bringing Carlos out of his coma today. She sounds pretty worried," I say.

"Yeah, there are a few things we should talk about before we get to the hospital," Brian says.

"What's that," I say, selecting fruit and a blueberry muffin from the platter in front of us.

"Chase called me this morning. The Larussio attorneys are fielding calls about Carlos's mental state before he got in the accident. It looks like Carlos's uncle, the one that lives in Italy, is trying to gain control of his financial power of attorney."

"I thought he had all that put in place before he was in the accident. Aren't Kate and Chase supposed to be handling all of his affairs?" I ask.

"They are, but her great uncle and uncle are contesting it."

"It's probably a good thing he's coming out of the coma then," I say.

"That's what we need to talk about. The teams are still trying to find out who was behind the accident. The only way to keep them from coming after Carlos and finishing what they started is to keep the public believing he's in a coma and not expected to live. It buys them a little time," he says.

"I won't say anything, but odd Kate didn't mention anything to me about it when we were talking," I say.

"I just got off the phone with Chase, so he may not have had a chance to discuss it with her," he says.

"I didn't mention anything about Ty's investigation to her. She's worried about her dad right now and I didn't have the heart to give her something else to fret about," I say.

"That's probably for the best, although it's sure to get out soon. We're trying to stay in front of the news releases, but there's a community fear factor with a murder of this magnitude."

"Hopefully we can keep it under wraps until her dad's out of the danger zone," I say as Matt walks into the room.

"Hi there stranger," I say.

"Hi there yourself," he says, his eyes twinkling. "Morning, Brian," he says.

"Jenny and I were talking about plans for the day," Brian says.

"Scottie just let me know that they're going to be moving Carlos and Karissa to a different unit," Matt says.

"Good, things are going as intended then. I just filled Jenny in on the plans for Carlos. We should probably leave for the hospital within the hour," Brian says.

"Okay, that should give us time to get a few things in place. I'll have it arranged," Matt says, immediately starting to text someone as he walks toward the elevator doors while Brian refills my coffee and fills me in on the transition of his chief operating officer position to Warren who he has been mentoring for the last month. Then Matt returns to let us know it's time to go. The drive through midmorning is bumper-to-bumper traffic, and other than the periodic blaring of taxicab horns, is uneventful. When we arrive at the hospital, Kate is in her mom's room curled up in a recliner with a white hospital blanket wrapped around her concentrating on her laptop. She starts to rise, but I intervene. "You look comfy. Stay there," I say, walking over to put my arms around her.

She looks up at me and I can tell she's trying to prevent tears. "How's your dad?" I ask.

"Not so good. They started decreasing his meds and the brain activity was all over the place. They didn't want him to have a seizure, so they had to give him a little more," she says.

"I'm so sorry," I say, taking a seat on the smaller straight-backed chair next to hers.

"Your father's a strong man, Kate. I'm sure he'll pull through this."

"Where are Chase and Don?" Brian asks.

"They're in Dad's room. The next one to the left as you walk out," she says.

"Matt, can you stay with the ladies? I need to talk to Chase for a few moments," he says.

"No problem," Matt says as Brian leaves the room to go and find the men.

"How is your mom taking all the news?" I ask.

"Not so well. She was awake earlier and you could see how excited she was, but when the physician told us what happened, you could just see her mentally shut down. They gave her some more pain medication for her back and shoulder and she's been asleep the last hour," she says.

"Just hang in there, Kate. Brian said they've got the best

medical care that money can buy and your father has a lot to live for."

"I'm trying. Right now I'm just so pissed that someone would do this. I want whoever put that hit out on my parents to pay," she says, fighting back the tears that threaten to spill.

"Can't say that anyone blames you for feeling that way," I say.

There's a brief knock on the door which Brian left slightly ajar. Matt opens it and immediately sends a text on his phone. The red-haired officer that questioned me yesterday and another I've never met start to enter the room and I walk toward them. "Gentlemen, can we go to the conference room and talk? I don't want to disrupt Kate and her mother," I say.

"I'm afraid that won't be necessary. Jennifer Torzial, you are under arrest for the murder of Ty Channing. You have the right to remain silent. Anything you say, can and will be used against you in the court of law. You have the right to an attorney. If you cannot afford an attorney, one will be appointed for you. Please place your hands behind your back," Officer Ryan says. My heart is racing and as soon as Matt finishes typing in another message he comes to stand beside me as they are applying the handcuffs.

I hear Kate's voice arguing with the men, but I can't really focus on what she's saying. My heart is pounding wildly and I can't help the tears that begin spilling.

Matt lifts my chin and places his arm around my shoulders. "I've already contacted Brian and Chase. We'll have an attorney meet you at the police station and get bail posted. Don't worry, Jenny," he says, brushing a slight kiss against my hair and wiping the tears from my face.

Brian stalks through the door with Chase right on his heels and takes in the handcuffs and the scene in front of him. "I've contacted my attorney. Don't say a goddamn word until he reaches you," Brian says.

I nod as the police officers escort me past the men and into the long corridor. It's like my mind is filtering things in slow motion. I can see nurses and doctors moving around their ledges and stations, but I can't really hear them. When we reach the hospital doors I am led outside of the building, to a black and white police car and put into the back. The door slams shut and the reality sets in as I see the strong black grid that separate the front and rear seats. Bumper-to-bumper traffic during the lunch hour in New York City makes the ride long and unpleasant. Every time I look up someone in an adjacent car is staring at me. It is unnerving and I sink lower in my seat.

When we arrive at the police station, the officer opens the back door and assists me out of the car and into the brick building, down a hall and into a central processing division. I'm told to take a seat across from a uniformed officer engrossed in paperwork. "Your name, date of birth and residence," he asks, looking up from his computer.

I answer his questions, but when he asks me if I have any gang affiliations that I wish to divulge, I roll my eyes toward the ceiling and almost laugh out loud. Now they think I'm a gang member.

He pauses briefly and clears his throat. "The question's routine ma'am. We want to make sure segregation isn't required. It's for your protection," he says, turning to the screen in front of him.

"Sorry," I say, realizing it's not this young man's fault that I'm here. The station is noisy and jam-packed with at least ten other desks identical to his, filled with people getting booked just like me. When we're finished the sergeant leads me down a hall and asks me to stand against the wall by a line that measures my height, and tells me to face the camera just before it flashes. This is what will be in the paper. This is what my mom and my family will see.

This will be the picture that accompanies the news story about the owner of Torzial being charged with murder.

"Well, well, well, looks like the princess has finally arrived," I hear and turn to look towards the beady-eyed officer that was so rude and disrespectful to me during questioning.

I don't have a chance to respond before another officer walks into the room. "Hey, just got a call from the big boss. The judge signed Torzial's bail release and it's already been posted. She's free to go," he says.

"How did that happen so quickly?" the beady-eyed one says to him.

"Didn't ask, apparently the order came straight from the top."

"Thank you," I say.

"You're welcome, ma'am. I'll walk you out to the front," the officer says. I glance at the beady-eyed one and his jaw is twitching, but he doesn't say a word.

I follow the officer through the doors and Brian is standing there, towering over another detective and the magnetism of his crystalline blue eyes pull mine toward his gaze. I almost run into his arms and he wraps them tightly around me. "Come on, you're going home, Sweetheart," he says.

Chapter 6

Brian

I'M TALKING WITH CHASE AND DON ABOUT CARLOS AND glance down at the incoming text from Matt.

Message: Police in our room. Arresting Jenny.

Fuck! I take a couple minutes to send instructions to my lawyer and to Scottie and then head into Karissa's room. The fuckers already have her in cuffs and Matt has his hands all over her. His arms are around her shoulders; he's kissing her hair and wiping her tears. It takes every bit of self-control not to go ballistic on his ass. We'll talk later. "Jenny, I've contacted my attorney. Don't say a Goddamn word until he reaches you," I say as they lead her away.

"I want someone behind that car keeping their eyes on her at all times," I say.

"Will do," Matt says.

"Not you, someone else," I snarl. He and Chase both raise their eyebrows at me, but I don't give a shit what they think.

"I'll make sure it's done," Matt says, heading out the door and down the same hallway they've led Jenny through.

"What the hell was that about?" Chase asks, but we are interrupted by my attorney calling. I answer the phone and listen. Thank fuck I have the best attorneys money can buy and they have best friends in all the right places. "Thanks for taking care of it so fast," I say before disconnecting.

"The judge will sign her out on bail and the money will be posted before she's done processing. I'm going to head over and pick her up," I say to Chase.

"Excellent news. Now would you like to tell me why you snapped at my security detail? I personally put him in charge of Jenny's security after she was raped. He was the only one besides Katarina that she talked to. She feels safe with him around," Chase says.

"He's off the case. Find him another fucking job," I say.

"Brian, you can't be serious. He's ...."

I cut him off. "I need to go. We can discuss it later. In the meantime, keep the fucker out of my way," I say, heading out of the room and down the hallway, texting Wes to have the car pulled around.

Traffic is always a bitch around this time and my patience is slim to none. I push the intercom. "Isn't there a faster way?"

"Not right now. Lanes should start opening up shortly," he says, and I resign myself for the lengthy ride across town, settle back into the seat and hit Scottie's number.

He answers on the first ring. "Learn anything?" I ask.

"We might have some good news."

"Tell me," I say in no mood to wait one more second.

"We knew Mancini wanted Ty dead but that Carlos Larussio's brother got to him first and left the Larussio markings. The police were sniffing around too much after his beating which left Mancini without a way to save face, or to show people what happens when they mess with the unions.

"Fuck! One, we'll never prove it if it was him or his group and two, even if we could it would mean a death sentence for Jenny and those involved," I say.

"Exactly, but I think we have, what do you Americans say, an ace in the hole?"

"I'm listening. Jay's intel team caught threads of a conversation. Apparently Mancini wasn't quick enough. According to intel someone got to Ty before Mancini did," he says.

"That doesn't sound any better to me."

"At first look, no. But, recall the way he was murdered. Poor lad left this earth with his willy down his throat. You see, that's Mancini's mark. The police must know its Mancini's mark and with his affiliations they'd be tied up in court for years, which is why they like Jenny for this. She's got ties to the Larussios who they think got to him the first time, she had motive and the trail leads right back to Carlos Larussio having someone kill the bloke for what he did to Jenny."

"She didn't do it and they don't fucking know what he did to her," I say.

"Find a little motive like her leaving his condo with a split lip and moving back into her own place the following day, set up the scene and voila! The arrest is made and the captain gets off everyone's back. A lot easier than going after Larussio or Mancini, especially if you're on the payroll."

"Fuck! So what are we doing about it?" I ask.

"Give us a little time, lad," he says.

"She doesn't have that luxury," I say.

"We're working on it as fast as we can, be assured of that Brian. We'll get it figured out. I'm using Jay's intel teams. They're seriously the best in the business."

"Sounds good. Have Jay give Chase a number so I can get even with him," I say before disconnecting as Wes pulls up in front of the police station. I don't wait for him to open my door or for the security detail behind us to get in stride as I head into the police station.

"I'm here to pick up Jennifer Torzial. She's been released on bail," I say to the short, dark-haired female behind the desk.

"All the paperwork has been sent over, she'll need to sign a few things to process out, but otherwise is free to go," she says, buzzing me through a set of double doors. I walk into the station office when the door clicks. There are desks filled with officers and people sitting across from them. Jenny walks through a door on the far side of the room accompanied by a policeman. Her eyes are downcast as they walk her into the room, but as though sensing me she looks up and rushes into my arms. I can feel her heart racing a mile a minute and hold her tight for a moment. "Come on, you're going home, Sweetheart," I say.

"The lady at the front desk mentioned paperwork," I say to the guy behind her.

"It's already been prepared and ready for a couple quick signatures, sir," he says, as we reach his desk. He starts to hand the packet to Jenny, but I take it from him and read the contents before handing it to her.

"It's okay to sign," I say, watching as she pens her signature in each of the areas that have been highlighted with a little yellow sticker.

When she's finished, I guide her out of the police station and into the awaiting limo. Wes navigates traffic back to my condo and she doesn't say a word, just stays buried in my arms. The silence is okay for right now, but I know her emotions are running high.

Wes pulls up to my sky-rise and the security detail opens the door for Jenny. I slide out the rear passenger door on the curb side behind her, placing my arm around her, guiding her past the doorman and into the private elevator that takes us to the penthouse. Two security men follow us in. She looks at each of them and doesn't say a word, but I know she must be wondering where Matt is.

We walk into the condo and when the doors close I turn her to face me. "We are going to get you out of this. I know you had nothing to do with his murder and we've got everyone possible working on your defense," I say, capturing her lips.

She kisses me back, opens to me and presses her body into my own. The only fucking thing I can do for her right now is to keep her mind off of what she's going through. I lift her into my arms and carry her into my bedroom laying her on the bed. She's looking at me with those come hither eyes. I want to dissolve every fucking worry on her face, every fear she has.

I slowly undress her, reveling in the perfection of her body. Creamy soft smooth skin, her nipples are bright pink and erect and I find it difficult to concentrate on anything else. I suckle one pert nub while caressing the other, rolling it between my thumb and forefinger. I hear her moan and know she feels it deep in her center. Her tits are so sensitive, she's fucking purring. I make a note to buy her a set of nipple clamps to adorn those beautiful tits.

She moans again and I know she's ready for me. I dip lower, kissing down her body, slowly removing her pants along with her undergarments. I'm not sure why she wears them around me. I want instant access, skirts and no panties. My cock twitches its agreement and I circle her mound with my tongue. Her hips rise and I smirk. She's more than ready, but I want her aching and begging for release. I graze her clit with my thumb and she moans softly. I want nothing more than to take it in my mouth and suck, but I restrain myself, licking just off the mark time and time again. Her hips rise and she's clawing at the sheets before I give in. Finally, I let my tongue wash over her over sensitized clit, just barely and she moans.

"Tell me what you want, Sweetheart," I say.

"Your tongue. God Brian, it feels so good," she says, writhing underneath me and my dick is having a hard time dealing with his wait, but all I want is for her to call my name when she's climaxing. I lick just off the mark and then again and she groans. I want her to beg me and she fucking does. "Brian, please," she moans, raising her hips into the air.

That's what I was waiting for and I capture her clit while I push two fingers inside of her. I know I hit her G spot when she starts purring and purring. She calls out my name again and I can feel her tensing up. She's getting ready to come. I suck her little clit hard, taking the entire nub into my mouth and she bucks with the explosion, calling out my name repeatedly. I wrap myself quickly, thrusting into her warmth, desperate to be deep inside of her. Her moan makes me pump hard, wishing I could feel her come around my own skin. I just need to feel her tight body wrapped around me. She starts moaning and I capture her cries with my lips, driving in deeper until I feel her clenching around me, almost there. I keep pummeling her G spot and she breaks from my kiss. "God Brian, it's so good," she moans and hearing her cry out my name while she's clenching around me pushes me over the edge and onto my own release.

I slip off and tie the condom and hold her in my arms. I keep waiting for the feeling to change. For me to get bored, for me to fuck her and then want her to leave, but I don't. I can't get past the helplessness I felt when they took her away from me and the thought of losing her is un-fucking-acceptable to me.

She's mine and I realize what's missing is for her to say something. Say that she cares, that maybe she loves me, but she doesn't. I've told her that she's mine, but she hasn't made that same commitment. I realize in that instant that maybe I've pushed her away too many times, maybe she's just been too hurt to care for someone else for a while.

Her hand in my hair pulls me out of my reverie. She pulls my lips to hers. "I love how you take care of me," she says.

I don't know exactly what I wanted to hear, but that's not it.

Chapter 7

Jenny

HE'S HOLDING ME IN HIS ARMS AND ALL I WANT TO HEAR IS that he loves me, that he cares and he doesn't say a word. I know he considers me his, but I don't have a clue what that really means. He likes submissives. Does that mean he just wants me as a submissive? I've read about them. The doms usually take care of their every need and the submissive role is to please them in and out of the bedroom. I know it makes me hot in the bedroom, and the way he's taking care of things for me with the murder accusations is making me believe it's what I want outside of the bedroom, too. I think I can try for Brian, but only if there are feelings on both sides.

I pull his lips close to mine. I need some sort of emotional connection to him after all that has happened. I don't want to scare him away by telling him how much I love him so soon, but I need him to know how much I appreciate being with him. "I love how you take care of me," I say.

He kisses my lips lightly and crawls out of bed, heading toward the bathroom. Nothing— not a trace of reciprocation. I hear the shower running and call Kate, desperately needing to talk to someone that really cares about me.

"God I was so worried about you. Chase told me that Brian got you out on bail, but all he would tell me is that you were questioned for Ty's murder and that they have very little in the way of evidence," she says.

"If Chase told you that, you know more than me. Brian and I haven't had a chance to talk much yet, but I know the officers who questioned me found out that I took a cab home from Ty's condo with a split lip and that was the last time we were seen together or that I was at his condo.

"I haven't seen any news releases yet. I thought with Torzial's connections to Prestian Corp and our relationship they would have it plastered all over the news. The paparazzi were at his place right away," I say.

"Yeah, I think they would have. Fortunately, Brian and Chase don't want it in the news and they pay a lot more than the newscasters receive for broadcasting it," she says, chuckling softly.

"When will I ever stop owing those two?" I say.

"Stop it. You don't owe anyone anything. We all know you're not guilty and Brian and Chase's teams are working around the clock to figure it all out. They're not going to let anything bad happen to you, Jenny," she says.

"Tell Chase thanks for me, would you?"

"I definitely will. Hey, I need to go. They're carrying Mom's dinner in and the physician is planning to stop by and check on my dad. They're going to try bringing him out of the coma again in the morning, but with a little smaller decrease in meds," she says.

"Okay, I hope everything goes well. I'll try to get over to the hospital as soon as I can."

"Sounds good. Jenny, try not to worry. They'll figure it out," she says before disconnecting.

Brian walks out of the bathroom with a towel wrapped around his waist. His hair is damp and there are still a few drops of water pebbling on his torso. I follow them down his abs to that sexy v-shaped line hidden from me by his towel. I look up and capture his sparkling blue eyes swirling with emotion.

"I just talked to Kate. She said that you and Chase are keeping the news crews at bay, paying them off to keep the arrest quiet," I say.

"Yeah, it wasn't very hard. They're just trying to make a buck like everyone else," he says, walking into his closet.

"Well thank you. I appreciate everything that you did to get me out, posting bail and keeping them from dragging my name through the mud," I say.

"It's nothing. I'd do it for anyone," he says.

I don't know what I expected, some sense of connection, but I guess that says it all from an emotional level. "I'll find a way to pay you back at some point. I need to go and visit my mom, let her know personally what's going on. Do you know where Matt is? I need to take him with me," I say, knowing I need time away to think about the situation and this relationship.

"He's been fired. If you need to travel and visit your mom I'll take you," he says.

"What?" I say, sitting straight up in bed.

"He's been moved to a different detail," Brian says.

"On whose authority did that happen?"

"I asked Chase to have him reassigned."

"Did you seriously think you were going to make life decisions like this for me? Maybe I wasn't clear and that's my fault. I love what you do to me in the bedroom and I do like how you take care of my needs outside of it, too, but some things are not your decisions to make."

He narrows his eyes at me and it infuriates me. "Matt is more to me than just a security detail. He's been with me night and day since Ty raped me. Do you know I couldn't even sleep or eat until Chase had him assigned to me full time? He's so loyal that he's given up his entire life to sleep on my couch just so I could feel secure every night. He means the world to me and if you don't call Chase and have him reassigned to me I will," I say.

His eyes are a deep smoldering blue and it's hard to understand the emotions swirling right now. He is quiet, too quiet, and for a moment it's like I can feel all of that pent up energy from across the room. "If that's how you feel then you should most definitely be together," he says, striding right out the bedroom door and slamming it behind him.

I get out of bed and walk right out into the living room. "What is wrong with you?" I say.

He turns toward me and looks my naked frame up and down. I ignore the heat of his stare. "Matt is my security detail. He and I have become close, because unlike you, I care about people and so does he."

"Yeah, he cares about you alright. He wants what's mine and I don't fucking share!" he says.

"Are you fucking serious? Do you even know anything about him? He's a fucking orphan Brian, like raised in foster home after foster home with no family. I love him like a big brother and I should have told him that," I say.

"Like a fucking brother?" Brian says.

"Yes, like the brother that I have, but was never there for me because he was too busy partying, getting high and making babies that he wouldn't ever take care of, a fucking brother, someone that loves me. Something you obviously know nothing about!" I yell, spinning and heading back into the bedroom and slamming the door behind me for good measure. I need to call Chase and find out where Matt is and have him reassigned. Ty is not a threat anymore. I am going home!

I call Chase and it goes to voicemail so I send him a text.

Message: Please reassign Matt to my security detail. Heading home. Will find a way to pay you back.

Reply: Stay where you are. It's not safe for you to be on your own. I will have Matt reassigned and have him pick you up at Brian's.

I pull on yoga pants, a cami, and my hoodie and then slip into my boots. I go into the bathroom and pack up a few of my personal belongings and throw them into my backpack. I'm not waiting for Chase and Brian to duke it out over Matt. I just need to get the fuck away from here where I can think straight.

I fully expect to run into Brian, but he's not in the living room or dining room and I breathe a sigh of relief. The elevator door opens and I get in, pressing the button for the ground floor. The door opens and I head across the reception area and towards the doorman and exit. "Have a great evening, Ms. Torzial," Ben says.

"Thanks Ben, you too," I say, heading out into the brisk winter weather. I pull my calf- length black down coat up a little closer to my chin and look around, spotting a cab just down the street. I've barely passed the door when two men grab my arms, painfully twisting them behind my back, and push me into a limo whose door opens like magic in front of us. "Get her in and let's go," I hear someone say.

Chapter 8

Brian

SHE'S DISTANCING HERSELF FROM ME AND I DON'T BLAME HER, but I don't know what the hell to say that changes it. "Matt is my security detail. He and I have become close; because unlike you, I care about people and so does he... he's someone that loves me. Something you obviously know nothing about!"

The words reverberate in my head over and over. She cares about him like a fucking brother? That's what this keeps going back to. She needs someone that cares about her. She told me that the first time we were together and I walked right the fuck out on her. I know that if I open that bedroom door, we are going to argue some more. She is mine and I am not fucking sharing her and fuck she's hot when she gets pissed at me. If I ever thought I wanted a submissive outside of the bedroom I was fucking wrong. God she makes my balls ache. Naked little body shaking with fury at me! Instead, I head to the gym and strip, pulling on a tank and gym pants from the closet.

When she said she was going to her mom's to tell her what was happening, one of the hardest things she'll probably ever need to do, and that she wanted Matt to go with her instead of me, I fucking saw red. I've told her she's mine and that I would take care of her. What doesn't she understand about that? I throw my headphones on and hit the treadmill.

About twenty minutes later my music cuts out and I see an incoming call from Scottie. "Lad, not sure what happened, but your lovey was on the run again. Perimeter security caught her coming out of the sky-rise, but couldn't get a shot off without hurting her.

"Get a shot off, what the fuck, Scottie?"

"She's been snatched, Brian. We've got security following the car and as soon as we know where they're heading we'll pick her up. I need to make sure before we do that you are okay with whatever comes down. We're dealing with the mafia, not sure at this point which one, but make no mistake you're going to be crossing the line of no return if we intercede," he says.

"Get her the fuck out of there Scottie. We'll deal with whatever happens," I say.

"Will do, lad, gotta go, be in touch soon," he says.

I get off the treadmill and hit the long red punching bag. It swings back at me and I hit it again, and again and again. Another half hour later I am drenched and just when I think I can't take the waiting anymore my phone buzzes.

"Brian here," I say.

"Lad, this is Scottie. I'm so sorry; they got her to one of the sky-rise helipads before our guys could figure out where they were going. I've already got Jay's team monitoring all outgoing aerials, but the reality is that we need to find her fast or we won't be able to. We have to find out which of the mafia groups grabbed her," he says.

I disconnect and hit the punching bag again and again and again. Son of a bitch! I call Chase's phone and he answers immediately.

"You heard? Someone's got Jenny," I say.

"I know Brian. Jay's got intel all over it, but we haven't received a call from them, yet. We don't know who we're dealing with. It could be the Italian uncle trying to use her as a means to control Katarina. Carlos put her in charge of the continued sale of his company assets to Vicenti and we know he's dead set against that and we also like him for putting the hit out on Carlos and Karissa."

"It could also be Mancini, right? Her company was the one that Ty used to launder his money and my understanding is that he wanted to off Ty as a means of showing his power, but someone else might have got to him first," I say.

"Yeah, Brian. There's also another possibility. Jay's intel team learned that Ty not only sold info to Mancini, but also to Mancini's enemies in Chicago. The Chicago family is not to be messed with. Mancini was out for Ty's blood to make him a lesson to anyone else that would cross him, but word on the street is that a Chicago enforcer got to him before Mancini did."

"Fuck, you mean Mancini was set up by someone in the Chicago family?" I ask.

"It's looking that way, Brian," Chase says.

"Then why do the police like Jenny for this?" I ask.

"You know why. She's connected to the Larussios and has a motive. They know they won't get a conviction otherwise," he says.

"Fuck!"

"Brian, we need to find out who and why they have her, develop an extraction plan, but we also need a long term strategy to mitigate the situation," Chase says.

I don't say anything. The gravity of the situation hits me so hard that I can barely breathe. I know what the mafia does to make people talk and I can barely hold down the nausea that overtakes me thinking about it. "Chase, we need the team together on this one," I say.

"Jay and Scottie are already working on it. They're plotting out strategies for each of the scenarios, but in all cases we're going to need Matt," Chase says.

"Need him for what?" I ask.

"Matt came to us highly skilled. We took him in, changed his name, his looks, and had a few tats removed, but he still knows how to navigate the Chicago mafia," Chase says.

"Holy fuck! He was one of them?" I say.

"Not only one of them, the enforcer. If anyone has a chance of getting Jenny back it's him. You good with this?" Chase asks.

"Yes, she loves and trusts the guy like a brother. I'll pay him whatever he wants," I say.

"Good, I'll connect with you later," he says.

I hit Scottie's number. "Did you know about Matt?" I ask.

"No lad. I'm running a background check on him as we speak, but trying to be extra careful so no one catches wind," he says.

"Do you know where he's at right now?" I say.

"I do. He's got a condo in town," he says.

I don't know why the fact that the fucker's still in the city surprises me. "I need the address."

He rattles it off and I punch it into my phone. "After Chase told him he was off the case Matt told him that he wasn't taking a different assignment until he heard it from her. When we found out she was taken Chase told him to sit tight."

I disconnect and send Wes a message to have the car brought around and head downstairs. Traffic isn't too bad tonight and we're able to make it across town in less than ten minutes. He pulls up in front of the building and lets me out. Security is following us and I know I should wait for them, but I don't fucking care.

The friendly inquisition of the uniformed bellman is an annoying delay. I answer his questions about me and the security team and wait with feigned patience while he announces me into his hand held device. "This way sir," he says, as he disconnects his device and swipes a badge over the magnetic pad and enters in a passcode.

The elevator opens into an impressive foyer of sorts and I knock on the only door I see. Everything's quiet but I know he's expecting me and bang on it again. "Matt, it's Brian. We need to talk, let me in," I say.

The door slowly opens and Matt steps back to allow me entry. He's dressed in faded blue jeans, a tight white t-shirt and no socks or shoes. I know Jenny thinks of him as a brother, but I don't know what this fucker thinks about her and I still have my suspicions.

"I came to apologize. I've been a fucking prick. I had Chase take you off Jenny's detail," I say.

"Come on in," he says, closing the door behind me. "Chase didn't come right out and say that, but after what happened at the hospital I figured as much," he says, taking a seat at the dining room table and gesturing me to the one across from him. The entire table is filled with New York maps, and different areas of the city are circled in green and red marker.

"What is this Matt?" I ask.

"All the safe houses that the Chicago Mafia and Mancini crew have here in the city of New York. The fuckers have places every-where," he says.

I whistle. "Shit, you think they're holding Jenny in one of these?" I ask.

"Look, maybe we should clear the air before I start rattling off all the secrets of the mafia," Matt says, turning his steely grey eyes at me.

"Yeah, you're right not to trust me. I don't know how I feel about you either after what I saw. Chase and Scottie seem to trust you and think you're the only way to get Jenny back, and so for that, I will pay you whatever you want and do whatever you ask. She's told me that she cares for you deeply, like a brother, but I don't know what your feelings are for her."

His eyes light up with grey blue amusement. "You fired me because you were fucking jealous?" he says, laughing out loud. It's a deep belly laugh and I want to punch him right in the mouth.

"I didn't say that. I told you she cares for you and I want to know if you've got your sights on her," I say, feeling like a fucking school boy.

"Oh, well by all means, let me set the record straight. You see, Chase and Jay put me in charge of Jenny after she was raped. Kate found out that she wasn't sleeping or eating. Chase asked me as a personal favor to him to move in with her. She offered me the upstairs guest room, but I stayed on her couch. You know, closer to the door in case the fucker came back," he says.

I nod. "She told me that and how secure she felt with you in the house, but you still haven't told me how you feel about her. I saw your arms around her, you kissing her hair. As you so aptly described, I'm a jealous fucker and I need to know how you feel about her," I say.

"You're fucking for real right? I love her, okay! She's like the little sister I never had but always wanted. I care about her, a lot, but let's get one thing straight. I don't love her like that."

I'm fucking elated and I can be generous now. "She cares about you a great deal, too. She was pissed off as hell that I had Chase let you go," I say.

"She was?" he asks, his eyes twinkling with amusement.

"I had a hundred and ten pounds of fury screaming at me and that's actually why she left the apartment without security. She said she loves you like a brother, like the one that she should have had. I guess her own wasn't much into responsibility with her or his wife and kids," I say.

"I met the douche bag when she went to see her mom and the kids before Christmas. He was high as a kite. Said it was the pain meds, but his accident was five years ago and I checked him out. He was arrested three times for possession with intent to sell and DUIs before his accident ever happened. He's got two precious kids that his mom is raising with money that Jenny sends to her."

"So will you take the job? Will you find her? I'll pay you whatever you ask," I say, knowing that he should tell me to go fuck myself because that's what I deserve, but he doesn't.

"Brian, I don't need your money. Chase makes damn sure that I'm paid well. I was going after her with or without your consent. Let me show you what I've drawn up and we can talk about how you can help," he says.

"I'm in," I say, scooting my chair closer.

"I've got all the safe houses outlined. I'm just waiting for them to land," he says.

"How do you know she's in the air?" I ask.

"I've got her wired, she just doesn't know it," he says, spinning his laptop around.

A small stick person is pulsing on the screen and her blood pressure is displayed digitally in the right hand corner. My respect for this guy keeps growing.

"You were always going after her?"

He smiles. "Damn straight. After the last stunt she pulled I needed to have a way to track her fast and to know when she was in trouble. Blood pressure is the best indicator. Don't worry, she knows everyone loves her and will be doing their best to get her back," he says.

I don't know about that after our argument, but I don't tell him that. "The bracelet she always wears and won't take off," I say.

"Yep, gave it to her when I was with her at her mom's before Christmas and made her promise me that she'd never remove it, no matter what. I've been tracking her with it," he says.

Chapter 9

Jenny

IN ONE MOMENT I'M PISSED OFF AND WALKING DOWN THE street to get into the cab and in the next second my hands are stretched behind my back and I'm forced into the back seat of a limo.

"Let's go," is all I hear before I'm smashed between two burly, smelly men in the back seat, a cloth is placed over my nose and I'm out.

"Get her onto the helicopter," someone says and I'm lifted and then placed on my feet. I struggle to regain consciousness and my balance, glancing around at my surroundings. We're on the top of a sky-rise in New York City and heading towards an awaiting helicopter. I no longer have my purse; someone must have taken it and my phone. I can't get a message to Brian or anyone. If they get me in that helicopter there's no way anyone will find me. The men in front of us are talking to each other and the big guy is practically dragging me.

"Please slow down," I say and the man slows a bit and turns to look at me. One little turn, that's all I need and as soon as it comes I take that moment to connect my knee with his groin.

"Bitch," he yells, letting go of my arm to clutch his crotch. I take off, back through the roof-top door slamming it behind me. No lock. I can hear them yelling and they're closing in. I can't wait for the elevator. It's the stairs or nothing. I can hear footsteps behind me and that propels me forward, floor after floor until I run right into the big burly chest of the man that I just kicked.

"Got her," he says into a two-way radio before placing it onto his belt. He pulls my hands tightly behind my back and pushes me down a few sets of stairs and then into the elevator. I should have known they would intercept me. He shoves me in and spins me around to face him as we ride back up to the rooftop. "Now let's try this again," he says, yanking me out of the elevator and toward the awaiting men and helicopter.

A man reaches down from the helicopter and just about drags me into the cabin. "Give me the rope. Not trusting this bitch again," my captor says, taking the length from the man in the copter and securing my hands tightly behind my back.

The other one laughs. "Quite the little hell cat you have on your hands, Nikko," he says.

"Yeah, let's hope she's as wild in the sack."

Nausea threatens, but I slowly force the feeling down. I need to keep a clear head. I let my mind wander back to some of the conversations I've had with Matt. When you can't do anything else take the time to gather information. Acquire every bit of detail about your abductors, memorize them. Listen to their conversations, store names and unique features in your mind for later. The big burly guy goes by Nikko. It's hard to hear after that as the blades start swirling and we lift off. I watch for landmarks below and in a matter of moments it's easy to tell we're flying over the Brooklyn Bridge toward Jersey.

The man sitting across from me has olive colored skin, dark hair, and deep brown eyes. He's watching his phone intently. Whoa, he's in dress pants and a sweater underneath his leather jacket. I look down at his socks and shoes- definitely Italian leather. The gold around his neck and watch on his wrist look like they weigh a ton. Whoever this guy is he has money. He feels me watching him and looks up, raising his eyebrows sardonically at me, and then just as quickly returns his attention to his phone. Nikko is sitting next to me and leans across the aisle to whisper something to the thinner one low enough that I am unable to hear.

The helicopter starts descending. We're somewhere in Brooklyn and then we land on a rooftop helipad. Nikko shoves me out of the helicopter and I barely land on my feet. I hope he has a permanent pain in his dick. "Get moving," he says, pushing me towards a door on the far side of the roof. The elevator door opens as we approach and we walk through. Nikko takes out his two way radio and instructs someone to bring the car around before the door closes.

The building is empty this late at night and we walk through a reception area to get to the front door. I'm trying to place the building. It's familiar, but I can't grasp the exact name or where in Brooklyn it is. Two Cadillacs are parked at the entrance and Nikko shoves me into the back seat of the first one on the street. "Get her to the house. We've got one more stop to make and we'll meet you there," he says to the driver.

I glare at him and he smiles. "I'll see you later sweetness," he says.

He raps on the hood of the car and the driver pulls into the street, turns a sharp corner and then merges with a lane of traffic. Too bad he tied my hands behind my back. If he had bound them in the front of me I could easily choke the asshole. I lean back in the seat and gauge the distance between my knees and feet and the seat in front of me. I need to act fast before we make it to the highway.

I pull my knees up to my chest and slowly lift my feet placing them right behind his seat. He hasn't noticed yet. I slowly slip them up and over, then quickly wrap them around his neck and squeeze, pulling back with all the strength that I have. He let's go of the steering wheel when I tighten my hold and I don't let up, crushing his neck as hard as I can between my crossed boots and the headrest.

The vehicle swerves, crossing into the other lane of traffic, bumping into the car next to us. There's blaring of horns and then suddenly he slams on the brake and using both hands forcefully pulls my legs apart. I am out powered and pull my feet back quickly, opening the door to scramble out while he catches his breath. I take off, weaving my way in between cars not waiting to see if he's behind me. "Help, please. Someone call 9-1-1," I yell.

The pounding of feet is getting closer and it's not long before hands on my shoulder spin me around. I cringe. The driver's face is beet red. "We're supposed to take you in alive, but you pull another fucking stunt like that and I'll shoot you in the leg," he says, grabbing me by the arm and marching me back to the car that he's left sideways in the middle of the road.

The driver of the car we hit is yelling. "Here, take this, get off the road and keep your fucking mouth shut," my captor says, throwing a wad of bills at the man. The guy looks down at the roll and peels the first hundred. "Looks good to me," he says, heading back to his car.

"Get in, cunt," he says, practically throwing me into the back seat before slamming the door shut. Sirens blare in the distance and he guns the engine, pulling in front of another vehicle that lies on the horn in protest before swerving around the corner and then making another quick right into a quieter residential area. He maneuvers the car for a few more blocks before he turns into a long driveway set off the street. As soon as we've entered the garage the door comes down and he hops out of the car.

"Get out," he says, grabbing me roughly by the arm, forcing me out of my seat, and pushing me ahead so hard that I nearly fall down the stairs into the basement below.

A couple of men are sitting at a square table playing cards and give me the once over when we walk through the door. "Brought us a little girlie action huh Benz," one of the men says.

"The cunt's all yours. Fucking pain in the ass. Nikko wants a piece of her first, but you can have a little fun with her until he arrives. Just make sure you keep her alive and pretty, those are the rules," he says, securing my tied hands to a hook on the wall before heading upstairs.

The older ruddy looking man's grey eyes haven't left my body. I feel a shiver of fear run down my spine and my heart starts beating faster as he approaches. "Boss wants to keep you pretty for Nikko, but he'd probably appreciate me giving you a little lesson on blow jobs, don't you think, Princess," he says, wiping his finger across my lips.

"Who are you and why am I here?" I ask.

"No, see we ask all the questions. I think I'll have to put something in that sweet little mouth of yours to keep you quiet," he says, running his fingers along my neck and past my collarbone, letting his finger dip over my nipple. He's leaned back slightly to get a good look at my face while he touches me. He thinks I'll cringe, but I don't. Instead my knee rises up and pounds him right in the crotch. I hear him suck wind and he doesn't even have enough air to say a word, he just drops to the floor holding his balls and gasping.

"Fuckin A," the other one says. He strides right over to me and brings his hand back. I prepare for a smack across the face, but he yanks it back at the last minute, restraining himself. "We'll deal with you later when you don't have to be pretty anymore," he says, extending his hand to the man still curled up on the floor.

"You gonna make it, Frankie?" he says, helping him into a kneeling position.

"Fucking bitch. Nice and slow, that's how your torture's gonna go," he says.

I don't say a word. If he had been just a little bit closer when he bent over to help his friend I could've kicked him in the face, but they're out of reach now, so I try to conserve my energy. When he looks up at me with those hateful grey eyes my nerves kick in. I focus on my breathing, trying to keep my heart rate from racing out of control as his friend leads him back to the card table.

There are footsteps upstairs. It sounds like a bunch of elephants running through the house. "Sounds like Nikko's back," the tall one says.

"Maybe he'll want some help with the little bitch," Frankie says.

"Probably be awhile. You know Nikko likes to draw it out with the ladies. Gets off on hearing them scream, but don't you worry once he gets done with you we'll have our turn," he says.

The nausea rises in my chest again and I have to physically swallow hard to keep it from rising.

Chapter 10

Brian

WE'RE IN THE CAR HEADING TO THE WATERFRONT HELIPAD closest to us. I can't keep my eyes off the fucking little stick person. It's the only way I know she's alive. We reach the Augusta, a helicopter known for its speed and air combat capabilities.

Matt shuts his iPad down. "Come on. I've got the app on my phone. They're heading toward Brooklyn," he says to the pilot.

"Roger that!" he says, lifting off and accelerating over the bay.

"Jay, there are three safe houses in Brooklyn. Can you have men stake them all out? I don't want to give these fuckheads any time at all with Jenny. I'll know exact locations once they get on the ground and can see which direction they head. In the meantime, we need a car and another team at the corner of Essington and sixth, there's a helipad there," he says into his walkie-talkie.

"Roger that, consider it done," Jay says over the two-way. When we get home Matt and I are going to have a serious talk about who he works for. I don't want Jenny's security left to anyone but him going forward.

The Augusta slices around the city lights of Manhattan and

turns toward Brooklyn. A helicopter is lifting off into the night right before we touch down. "Jay, can you get intel on a copter just lifting off? ID number is NTJ320."

"Yep, we'll have it run ASAP."

"Fuck," Matt explodes beside me. "Jenny just took off running. Where the hell is she

going? She's running downhill. The stairs— she's on the fucking stairs! Christ, she just came to a complete halt, but her heart's pounding. I need ground visual," he yells into his walkie-talkie.

"Our team just spotted her coming out of the building, but they've got her heavily secured," the voice on the other end says.

"Don't lose her, we don't know why they took her yet so we can't be sure they'll keep her alive if push comes to shove."

I swallow down the vile taste in my mouth. Fuck! "Keep me posted. We're heading down. Just keep the car out of sight, but don't let the other team lose her," Matt says.

"Things might get a little ugly, Brian. I'd rather not put you in the line of fire," he says and right there I cut him off. "I'm going with you. Let's move," I say.

"Hold up then. Put this on," he says, tossing one of the vests from the Augusta at

me as we land. I shrug off my jacket and slip it on over my shirt. You know how to handle a piece?" he says, pulling out a Glock.

"Only at the range, but I know how to pull a fucking trigger if I need to," I say.

"Let's go," he says, leading the way to the rooftop elevator. We're heading to the side where the car is parked," he says, gesturing me to keep quiet.

I nod, following his lead out of the elevator and into the back seat of a black Lincoln. The driver and another man in the front seat acknowledge Matt. "How many teams are in place?" he asks the men, all the while keeping his eyes on is phone.

"We've got three teams in..." he starts to say, but Matt cuts him off. "We've got trouble. Her heart rate is going off the charts. Where the fuck is she? I need eyes on the ground, Jay!" he yells into his two-way.

"Matt they put her in the back seat of a car with only a driver up front. They're making their way down fourth street. They have a vehicle full of security behind them or we would have gotten her already," Jay says over the radio.

"Something's fucking happening, right the fuck now," he grinds out. "Shit, shit, shit, Now she's running. All eyes on that fucking car!"

"We've got a team on the street and just caught sight of her. He's got her at gunpoint, Matt. We can't take him out. He's not going to kill her or he would have done it already," Jay says.

That's no reassurance to me. I am about to lose my fucking mind! We watch the green stick person on Matt's phone and can see when she stops. The car starts driving again, the little stick moves with it, turning in and out of streets until Matt knows exactly which safe house they're taking her to.

"Jay it's the one off ninth street. They'll be there in less than five minutes; we're about five behind him. Can you run ops- I need to be on the ground," he says.

"You got it, Matt. We'll have the element of surprise, and no one will put her in harms way," Jay says over the walkie-talkie.

"Jay, I want at least two of the fuckers alive. As soon as we get her out of there I want them secured," he says.

"Consider it done," Jay says.

I look up at Matt and he avoids my eyes, looking down at his phone and we both turn our focus to the stick person on the screen. Her heart rate is pretty stable and she's walking slowly.

The car pulls up to stop and Matt opens the door. "Stay behind me. Whatever you see, stay put. Do not try to be a hero. You'll only put her in jeopardy. Our teams do this for a living, they know exactly what to do and what not to do, okay?" he says.

"Say no more, I've got it," I say, following behind him. We're carefully making our way from bush to bush, yard to yard until he stops suddenly.

"Jay, her heart rate's going through the roof, get them in there," he says.

"They're in the garage and have all the exits surrounded. Give me two minutes," he says.

"Roger that," Matt says, pushing us forward, holding up his hand to be quiet as we reach the house. "Let's go around the back, they've got her in the basement. There's a stairwell there."

I don't know how the fuck he knows that and have no time to think about it as a car on the street revs its engine loudly against the quiet of the night.

"We've got her. Three dead and three alive. I'll let you take it from here," Jay says.

"Roger that," Matt says, leading me in through the back door and down a flight of steps to a basement. We walk in and one of Jay's team is untying ropes that bind Jenny's wrists. I want to fucking murder someone right the fuck now. As soon as she's freed she practically runs into my arms and I hold her tight.

"Jenny, I need two men that you think have the most information. Who do we take?" Matt asks.

She points out two men. "You also want Nikko. He's not here, but should be back shortly," she says.

"He was probably warned off, but we'll try to find him," he says.

"That would be good," she says.

"Get her to the car. The men will take you both back to your place," Matt says.

I put my arm around Jenny and two of the security detail leads us out to the car that has now pulled up in front of the house. The guard opens the back door and I close it after Jenny is safely inside, walking around the back of the car and getting in beside her.

"Who are they Brian? What do they want with me?" she asks as the driver navigates the residential area until we are back on the highway.

"We don't know yet, Sweetheart, but Matt's going to find out," I say, pulling her into my arms.

"I thought you fired him," she says, looking up at me with those wide green eyes.

"I did Sweetheart, but I was wrong about him. I want him permanently assigned to you going forward," I say.

She burrows deeper, nuzzling into my chest while I send a message to Chase to let them know we're heading home and that Matt is working to find out who the fuckers are.

Message: Glad to hear all is well. Take care of her.

Reply: I want to know who the fuckers are as soon as you do.

Message: Matt wanted to handle things personally. He'll let us know.

Reply: Has Jay been connecting with Scottie?

Message: Yes, they're working together. Scottie has new leads.

I look down at Jenny. She's safe, secure and once again asleep against my heartbeat. I kiss the top of her hair. There's nothing that I won't do to keep her safe and I can't wait to find out what Matt learns. I hit Scottie's number and he answers right away.

"Hey lad, glad we've got your lass back," he say.

"Chase said you might have new info?" I say.

"No, he just learned what you already knew, but I do have one update that I didn't share with him," he says.

"What's that Scottie?" I say.

"Can you call me back on the secure line?" he says.

"Give me a minute," I say, disconnecting and redialing. "What did you find out?"

"I started an in-depth profile on Matt after you fired him. It looks like you may have been right about him. Brian, he used to be the enforcer for the Chicago mafia. If our teams can figure it out so can others. Technology has changed so much in the last few years. They covered all their tracks with documentation and identifying records, but one thing you can't change nowadays without surgery are your prints and facial recognition," Scottie says.

"Fuck! Find out everything you can and then figure out what it's going to take to hire him on full-time. I want him assigned permanently to Jenny and anything else that comes up," I say.

"Happy to oblige lad," he says before disconnecting.

I've got two messages from my lawyer asking me to call him as soon as possible. I hit his contact number and he picks up in one ring.

"Brian, I've been trying to get ahold of you," he says, seemingly out of breath.

"I see that. I've been a little busy," I snap.

"Sorry to be the one to tell you this Brian, but things aren't looking good. They found strands of Jenny's hair on the jacket Ty had on the night of his murder," he says.

Chapter 11

Jenny

THE SOUND OF NIKKO'S NAME PARALYZES ME. SOMETHING IN his eyes sends fear right down my spine.

Frankie is sitting at the table, still clutching his balls. I hope the damage is permanent. His partner goes to the refrigerator and gets some ice, wrapping it up in one of the dish towels sitting by the sink.

"Here, use this," he says to Frankie, handing him the home-made ice pack.

The footsteps upstairs are loud, but apparently that's normal since the guys at the table pay little mind to it. All of a sudden processions of quiet popping sounds fill the air. The guy sitting across from Frankie runs toward the staircase, but it's too late. He's stopped short by a quick procession of gunfire. He falls back screaming and clutching his leg. Frankie goes for his weapon.

"Gun," I yell and just like that someone overtakes him.

"Put it down or you die mother fucker," a tall man I don't recognize says, pointing a long-ass rifle in my captor's face.

He places his pistol on the table and the man with the rifle

73

takes it into his possession and makes quick work of securing the tall guy's hands and feet.

One of the men walks over to me. "Let's get you untied," he says, cutting the ropes that are securing me to the wall. He's just removed them from my wrists when Brian and Matt begin walking down the stairs. I fly across the room toward Brian the moment he hits the bottom step and he scoops me into his arms.

"Jenny, I need the men you think will have the most information. Two men. Who do we take?" Matt asks.

I point to the two that have been holding me prisoner. "You also want Nikko. He's not here, but should be back shortly," I say.

"He was probably warned off, but we'll try to find him," Matt says.

"It would be good if you could take him out," I say and I mean it. Something in his eyes were the same as Ty's. He wants me dead or tortured and I shiver just thinking about it.

Brian's arms go around me and he guides me upstairs to the car and in a matter of minutes we are in the back seat, he has his arms around me, and we are on the way to the condo. I snuggle in next to him. It's the only time I feel safe and it's the only time I can sleep.

"Sweetheart, wake up," Brian says, lifting me into his arms and out of the Lincoln sometime later. I groggily rouse and look around taking in my surroundings as he carries me through the lobby.

"Brian, I'm good. I can walk," I say, feeling self-conscious with all the security detail joining us in the elevator.

"Shh, Sweetheart. You can go back to sleep in a few minutes," he says, carrying me out of the elevator and into the dining room, dismissing security after he thanks them.

I don't want to sleep. All I want is his arms around me and to hear him say I love you, three simple words that would mean the world to me. He wants me for his own, he's made that clear, but love, he's just not capable of it and he's made that pretty damn clear, too. "It's only eight. Too early to go to bed for the night. A short nap was all I needed. I think we should talk," I say as he puts me down.

"Glass of wine?" he asks, getting a bottle out of the wine refrigerator.

"Yes, please," I say, watching him as he pours a glass of sweet red for each of us and hands me one. I swirl it, inhaling the aroma and sip. He is every bit as much a wine connoisseur as Carlos Larussio.

"What's on your mind, Jenny?" he asks, watching me warily from beneath his glass. He's going to let me drive the conversation and I find that oddly intimidating even though I am the one that started down this path.

"I really appreciate that you and Matt came after me, but I'm confused. What happened between you guys? I was shocked to see you both walk into that room together. I never expected to get out alive after they got me into the helicopter. When Karissa was abducted Kate told me a lot about what happens in kidnapping and human trafficking cases. I seriously didn't expect to get through it," I say.

His jaw is twitching and he nods, seemingly contemplating. "I was an asshole. I saw Matt holding you in his arms at the hospital and had him removed from your detail without knowing all the facts. I assumed he wanted you for his own and didn't take the time to find out his real feelings."

"And what, the light just suddenly came on? You've got to give me something here, Brian. I told you I didn't think of him like that, but you didn't believe me? What happened? All I know is when I left he was off my detail and the next thing I know you both storm the place. How did you even know how to find me?"

"The last time you were this angry with me you were naked. I liked that better," he says, smirking over his wine glass.

"I guess I got a little heated, but you're still not answering my questions," I say.

"A little heated? Sweetheart you were naked, furious and fucking hot and all I could think about was putting you over my knee and watching your perfect little ass turn pink."

My center clenches and I feel myself moistening. "You didn't answer me," I say, knowing I'm just baiting the tiger as I take a sip of my wine.

"Because you're mine and I couldn't stand that fucker touching you."

I love that he wants to own me in bed and while most of me, the horny me, wants to submit to whatever he wants, there's a part of me that can't because I need the emotional connection. "Brian, what does being yours mean? What does it mean to you?" I say.

He takes a sip of his wine, contemplating my question. The look in his eyes is intense and makes me nervous. "It means that I want you for myself, that I'm not sharing you and that I want to be the one to take care of every need that you have and protect you," he says.

I'm not sure why I was hoping for something that clearly didn't exist. I nod. "You've said that before. You still want a submissive with no emotional strings. I thought that type of relationship might work between us. The sex is amazing, incredible actually, and my feelings are so strong that I thought I could, but I can't. I need someone that actually cares about me outside of the bedroom. I guess I want the kind of relationship girls dream about. Maybe I could be convinced to enjoy you for the short-term though," I say, cringing inside at the tightening of his jaw.

"Well, you're in luck Sweetheart because I no longer have an interest in having you as my submissive. I've had a taste of that and it's not exactly what I'm looking for," he says.

I take a sip of my wine. Arrogant asshole! I thought it would be hard, but I didn't expect to feel the pang of hurt or jealousy hearing his words caused. "Why even rescue me? What were you looking for, Brian? A few more romps with someone like the bimbo on your computer the other night?" I say, taking a large sip of wine and refilling my glass from the bottle on the table.

He raises his eyebrows in question and stands up. His jaw is twitching and his crystalline blue eyes are like ice. I can tell that I've pushed him too far. "You've misread the signs," he says, grasping my hand in his and pulling me toward the bedroom.

"Wait, this isn't what I want Brian," I say, trying to pull away, but his rock-hard strength doesn't allow it.

He pulls my body closer and grasps my neck under my hair with one hand while the other hand on my lower back pulls me close. "Now it's my time to talk and your turn to listen. I need more, too. You're right. I do want to hear you tell me, "yes sir," in the bedroom and scream my name when I'm fucking you and spanking your little ass until it turns pink, but while it's true I do need you submissive in the bedroom, I want more, too. I intend to have your hot little body pressed against me every night and wake up every morning watching you sleep in my arms because when I said you were mine, I meant it. You are fucking mine, today, tomorrow and forever. I love you, Sweetheart," he says, kissing my lips lightly with his.

Chapter 12

Brian

"I LOVE YOU, TOO, BRIAN," SHE SAYS AND I CRUSH HER LIPS with mine, exploring her depths as she opens for me. She tastes so sweet and the realization that she is all mine, and loves me washes over me. I want to mark her in the worst way, but I can't drag my lips from hers for a few minutes. When I finally do my tongue finds the sensitive skin behind her ears and the sounds of her purring makes my dick ache with longing. I continue suckling her, feasting on the creamy white skin of her neck while we undress. I know she'll have marks tomorrow, my marks, and I know it's juvenile, but I don't fucking care.

Her tits are the most gorgeous things I have ever seen. The erect pink little nubs poking out are just aching to be sucked on and I take one between my lips while rubbing the other one between my finger and thumb. I squeeze harder and she moans. I slip my hands beneath her white lacy panties, the only thing left covering her from me. I find exactly what I want. God that thick sweet center. I run my finger through its depths and across her folds pressing over her clit.

She moans again and I love that sound, but by the end of this night I want to hear her scream my name. I move lower, continuing to rub her nipples while I caress her belly with my tongue. She squirms, she knows where I'm going and she arches her hips trying to hurry me. I smirk to myself. Not on your life Sweetheart, I'm going to make you beg. I circle around her navel and lower, caressing her smooth silky mound. Her fingers dig into the sheets at her sides and her ass tightens as I finally let me tongue wash over her sensitive little nub. "Brian," she moans and my dick twitches hard.

"This pussy is mine," I say, circling her clit while finding the sensitive little rosebud of her ass. She tenses as she feels my thumb there. "I'm going to make you scream tonight." I moisten it with her wetness and circle her until she's squirming beneath me, pressing slightly just to keep her level of anticipation up and her responsiveness makes it hard not to thrust my throbbing cock deep inside of her, but tonight is for her. I continue gently caressing her clit with my tongue and press slightly into her ass with my thumb. She moans in response and her body grips me like a vice. She's so tight and all I can think about is how her tight little ass will feel around my cock once I've trained and stretched her. I leave my thumb, still letting her acclimate to the intrusion, but when I take her clit in my mouth and suck, she moans louder and I let it penetrate her fully, moving it in and out, trying to find that exact spot. I know when I hit it, because she rises up, and her hands start clawing at the sheets. "Brian," she screams.

I don't stop because I want her to ride out that orgasm completely before I start building her next one. Her hot body is still trembling and my dick is throbbing as I raise her arms over her head. "Taste how sweet you are," I say, licking her lips before capturing them, exploring her depths with my tongue. She moans as I continue my exploration and apply the soft suede black leather straps and silver buckles to her dainty wrists. "Trust me?"

Her eyes are glazed over and she nods. "I need to hear it Sweetheart."

"Yes," she says.

I'm going to push her boundaries and drive out every fucking horrible memory she's ever experienced and I know that's exactly what she wants and needs. "Yes, what?" I say.

There it is, the tipped up curve of her sassy lips and my dick twitches before I even hear her response. "Yes, sir," she says and I gently affix her to the headboard.

"Good girl. Now you get to decide, feet bound or not?" I say, knowing I need to give her the time she needs.

"Whatever pleases you," she says without hesitation, looking up at me with those deep green eyes.

Fuck me! I instantly feel the pre-cum leaking from my aching cock. She thinks I am the one with all the control, but we will only ever do what she wants and needs, and I know being fully restrained and allowed to explore her sensuality is one of her deepest desires.

"Good girl. Knees up and let your legs drop to the sides," I instruct.

She obeys immediately and her belly tightens and I know right then that she feels it all the way in her center. I take a moment to stroke my cock, squeezing hard at the base to stem the tidal wave that is ensuing. I reach for the matching ankle cuffs and hold them up for her to see. Her sharp intake of breath and the way she licks her lips is such a fucking turn on.

"Use your safe word if you need to," I say, buckling one to each of her ankles. I take a moment to admire her demure look before I finish affixing each of the restraints and contemplate the look in her eyes. She's flushed, her breathing is erratic and her eyes are filled with lust. I spread her legs and my dick hardens at the sound of my name in her cry as her legs are opened wide apart for me.

"Brian!"

"Scream all you want. This is for your pleasure," I say, pushing her legs up towards the headboard. She's panting and when I look down I want to stick my dick right into that pooling honey pot. Shit she's wet and creamy for me and her opened pussy is every man's wet fucking dream.

I somehow maintain my focus and attach the ankle cuffs to the same hooks that her wrists are affixed to. Now I have complete access to both holes, but I wait to see how she acclimates, needing to know she wants to be restrained in this position and wants to accept the pleasure I can give her. She's fantasized about it, but that's different than experiencing it.

I am holding my breath waiting for her cue and she fucking moans my name. She knows I won't hurt her, she trusts me with her desire. God, I've never been so turned on. Fuck me! I want to make her scream over and over again tonight. I want her to know the power of being in control of her every sexual desire. I love her in this position, opened for me, immobile by her own want. I can't wait any longer to taste the honey that's pooling in her center. I stick my tongue inside and she moans while my dick twitches. I caress her clit with my tongue and she thrashes around.

I've taken away her ability to move and I know I need to keep checking on her emotionally. "Your legs are spread wide open for me. I can see you dripping for me, is that what you like?" I ask.

She fucking moans in response and writhes against her handcuffs. "I need words. Yes, no or safe word Sweetheart," I say.

"Yes! God, it's so good, Brian," she pants.

I need no further invitation than that. I graze a very small, but lengthy dildo against her wetness and then let it slide down to her rosebud. I am going to enjoy training her slowly. She loved my thumb and I can't fucking wait to bury my cock in her ass, but it will take time. I drizzle lubricant on her and watch her eyes fill with lust as I press the small device against her opening. "You liked my finger, this is slightly larger. Can you take it?" I ask.

She nods. "I can try," she says.

It's not the "yes sir," that I usually demand, but for some reason it's so much fucking more.

I rub it along her seam and wetness before pressing against her a little more firmly. I feel her stiffen and hold it still, right at the entrance. I could drown in her eyes, they are wide and dilated. "If you don't safe word now, your chance will be gone," I say.

She shakes her head from side to side. "I want this," she moans and I press forward, but slowly, giving her anal ring time to adjust to the intrusion. I lean down and suckle her clit while it's stretching her and she tries to rise up, but her binds hold her still.

"Like this Sweetheart?" I ask, taking my mouth off her clit for just a moment to look up at her.

"Brian, I want to come again so bad," she pants and I use that moment to suck her clit hard and slide the small dildo fully into her ass, gliding the smooth wet surface in and out.

Her breathing begins to change and her hips rise, wanting more and I use the handle of the vibrator to bring her to a slow and burning frenzy.

"Brian, don't stop!" she screams, bucking as best she can against my mouth and I suck her as hard as I can while she's thrashing against her restraints and screaming my name.

Her climax peaks and I watch in awe as her body trembles in front of me.

"Is that what you like, what you read about, what you fantasized about?" I ask.

She does not hesitate in her response. "Yes, sir," she says.

Fuck me and now I want nothing more than to show her who

is in charge of her orgasms and I am not by any means done listening to her scream my name.

I leave the small plug in her ass and lock it into place. It will continue to train her and I run my finger down her slit. Damn it, she's so fucking wet and slick. I rub the bulb of my cock against her entrance, so wet, smooth and silky. As much as I want to push in and take what's mine I need her assurance. "Tell me what you want right now," I grind out.

"I want you, deep inside of me," she says.

Fuck! I press my cock past her entrance reveling in her heat and for once in my life lack the ability to hold back. I drive into her deep, hitting that special little button of hers that I have come to know so well. It is difficult for her to move in this position, but her body rises as much as it can meeting me thrust for thrust.

I reach between us and hit the button to start the vibration on the plug in her ass. She fucking moans and I can barely keep it together for one more minute. I squeeze hard at my base, willing myself to hold back to allow her this pleasure. The vibrator is creating a rhythmic pull and I can feel it inside of her against the length of my cock. She bucks against me and I drive deep, over and over again as the feel of the dildo vibrating against my cock and her screams of "Brian, don't stop," reverberate in my ear until I feel her tightening around me.

"Come for me, Sweetheart," I say and she does, clenching my cock like a vice as she trembles around me and only then do I allow myself the release that has been building and building and seems to go on forever. I remove the toy and reach up to free her, pulling her into my arms, wanting to feel her against my chest as she comes down. Her heart rate is finally returning to normal and I'm still running my hands along the curve of her delectable spine. She's looking up at me with those hazy green bedroom eyes. "You meant what you said," she says.

"Sweetheart, I never say what I don't mean," I say, pushing the hair out of her eyes.

"I love you," she says, reaching up to kiss my lips. Three little words, the ones I've never wanted to hear, but that I could spend a lifetime listening to coming from those lips.

"I love you too," I say and the realization of just how much I do makes me swallow hard as I think about the situation swirling around us. "Can you sleep now?" I say, spooning her warm body into my own.

My cell buzzes and I glance at the time, eight in morning.

"Scottie, slow down," I say, pushing the volume on the side of my phone down as low as it will go, but Jenny's already awake.

"All slept out. Jumping in the shower," she mouths to me and heads into the bathroom. She is completely nude and my hard dick twitches as I watch her walk into the bathroom and close the door.

"Jay just called. We weren't dealing with Mancini's crew. The old world Chicago family is after him. He's certain they took Ty out of the picture using Mancini's modus operandi to set him up."

"They can kill each other for all I care. What the fuck does it have to do with Jenny?"

"Brian, Matt will be on his way back to your condo as soon as he can. He wanted to tell you himself but Jay pulled it out of him. They took Jenny because of her ties to Mancini."

"Bullshit!"

"The two men were interrogated separately and both said the same thing, but neither knew what the business was, or had anything to lose thinking they were dead at that point."

"Matt's positive about this?" I say.

"He told Jay there was no way either of them was lying," Scottie says.

"Fuck."

"I'm sorry, lad. Matt will fill you in more later tonight. He's got some loose ends to tie up but will be over around eight and in the meantime Jay's already got his intel teams looking into it."

"Fuck," I say again, disconnecting and running my hand through my hair.

Chapter 13

Jenny

IN A MATTER OF DAYS MY LIFE HAS BEEN TURNED UPSIDE down again and I blame Ty for it all. Whatever he did caused his murder and I don't regret that he's gone. Maybe I should, but I don't. In fact, I feel somewhat vindicated and I know that attitude is not going to help me in court.

I still don't have a clue who snatched me and how Matt and Brian came together to get me out, but I know he loves me and he'll tell me the rest at some point. I step out of the shower and spritz on a little of the aloe mist that Kate bought for me when she was in Aruba on her anniversary trip. It locks in moisture and gives my skin a smooth and sleek look. I blow-dry my hair and slip into the short little satiny robe that Brian had his shopper purchase for me, tying the sash and turning to look in the mirror. It covers all the necessary spots, but the thin material doesn't leave much to the imagination.

Brian is sitting up in bed and I slide in next to his warmth and kiss him. "We need to talk, Sweetheart," he says, returning my kiss before pulling me into his arms and onto his lap.

"That was Scottie on the phone. The men who kidnapped you are part of the Chicago mafia, the old world family, not Mancini's crew," he says, watching me intently.

"Two different families?" I ask

"Mancini was working for them, but word is he was embezzling and had his own crew running on the side. They're in a war over one of the districts in Chicago," he says.

"Brian what do they want with me? I mean my company is based in Chicago and that's where I live, but other than that I don't know how I fit into all of this."

He nods. "Matt interrogated the two men that were holding you captive. They told him they were given orders to take you because you were in a business relationship with Mancini, their rival," he says.

"What the hell! Brian, I had no clue who he was until you mentioned his name before the cops questioned me," I say.

"Scottie was able to find out the police have an email between you and Mancini. They're holding it close to the vest for now, but he has a copy. It hasn't even made it to the evidence room. Someone on the police payroll is intentionally withholding evidence and he's trying to find out who they're working for."

What didn't he understand? I narrow my eyes at him and get out of bed. "You're not hearing me, Brian. The police couldn't have an email between Dominic Mancini and myself because it doesn't exist," I say, barely hanging on to my composure.

"I asked Scottie to get us a copy of what they have so we can take a look at it," he says appearing so cool and collected about the whole thing that it just pisses me right off.

"And just why would you do that, unless you don't believe a word I've told you?" There's a brief hesitation, a pause and that's when I know. He doesn't know what to believe. He doesn't trust me. I undo the tie of my robe and let it drop to the ground. "I need to find Matt. He will believe me and get to the bottom of this," I say, whirling around and heading to the dresser.

I have barely pulled out a pair of yoga pants and sweatshirt before he turns me to face him. "Don't try to make me jealous to get your way. I won't be manipulated."

"You don't trust me!" I say, desperately trying to hold back the tears and hurt.

"I trust you, Sweetheart. This isn't about that, it's about getting to the bottom of this mess and what I told you is true. The police have an email between you and Mancini, whether it's real or not that's what they have," he says, raising my chin to his face so I have no choice but to look into his smoldering blue eyes.

I am trying hard to hold back the tears of frustration. "How the hell am I supposed to fight this when everything keeps pointing towards my guilt?"

"You don't. You let me handle it. You trust that I will get you through this," he says, capturing my lips and all thought of argument is lost as he scoops me up and places me on the bed before lying down beside me.

"While your behavior requires punishment, I think we'll save that for another day. Right now all I want is for you to know how much you mean to me and let me take care of things, understand?" he says, caressing my cheek with his hand.

I nod, overcome with the emotions of the last couple days and enormity of everything happening.

"I need words?" he reminds, kissing my lips gently.

"Yes, I'll let you take care of everything and I'm sorry I didn't think you believed me," I say, rubbing his strong jawline with my finger.

The blue in his eyes clears right in front of me and he smirks. "You're forgiven, but that's not going to keep your ass out of trouble for that little outburst. I plan to have a sore hand from bending you over my knee and spanking your delectable little ass," he says.

"I like the sound of that," I say, softly kissing him on the lips.

"And it turns me right the fuck on that you do," he says.

"I know you're taking care of everything but I can't help feeling like there's something you're not telling me and it must be bad," I say.

He sighs. "I was waiting to tell you until we know a little bit more, but your hair was found on the jacket Ty was wearing when he was murdered. Logically, you lived in his condo and your hair could have settled there. I've got Scottie and Larry trying to put together the defense as we speak."

"It just keeps coming back to me over and over," I say and he pulls me closer.

"We'll get to the bottom of it. Larry is the best attorney in his field or he wouldn't be working for Carrington Steel. I have no doubt he'll create an effective reasonable doubt about the hair, but we need to find out how the letter originated from your computer IP address if you didn't send it," he says.

"Wait, wait. The day that Ty was in my condo, he said he was planting evidence that would make me look guilty for all the money laundering. I never even gave it another thought because you and Matt spoiled his plans. He never got the chance to finish what he was in my apartment to do and when Chase found out he was laundering money through Torzial, he had Jay and his team completely wipe my computer and any evidence of the money going through Torzial. I thought it was all taken care of," I say.

He sits up in bed resting against the headboard pulling me with him. "He either found a different way to get it loaded or had someone do it remotely. That's what we need to figure out. The way Ty was killed was Mancini's trademark, but the hard truth of the matter is that the police know they won't be able to make anything stick to him or the mafia. You were his girlfriend, broke up on bad terms with a documented busted lip, he ends up battered with the Larussio markings and you're best friends with Larussio's daughter."

"So they're trying to pin this on me because they can't convict the real criminal?" I say.

He pulls me close and kisses the top of my head. "I'm not saying it's right, and maybe we've got it wrong. The police are trying to wrap this up fast for the community and in all fairness to them they probably think they have the right person."

"It just keeps getting worse and worse. I feel like my life is spinning so out of control and there's nothing that I can do to prevent it," I say.

"There's one thing that you can do," he says, pulling me to sit aside his powerful thighs.

"What's that," I say, laughing as I catch my breath and regain my balance hanging onto his shoulders.

"When I said let me take care of things, I meant relinquish all control, stop worrying, that is my job and if I have to tell you again I'll have to devise a wicked punishment for you. One that you won't enjoy as much as the others you've experienced," he says.

I lean in and kiss his lips. "I love you and need you to take control, want you to take control," I say.

Chapter 14

Brian

I COULD LISTEN TO THIS WOMAN SAY THOSE WORDS ALL DAY long and never tire of it. "Good then from now on you don't worry, I do that all of that," I say.

She nods. I don't tell her that I'm just as anxious as she is to talk to Matt and find out exactly what happened after we left and I don't have a fucking clue what he's up to that's going to take him all day. If he's right and the Chicago family was behind the kidnapping, this isn't over for a long shot and we've just stepped into something much bigger than us.

"You need to finish getting ready and I need a shower," I say, grabbing her by the waist and hauling her to my body for one last kiss. Her eyes are bright and lively and her soft pink lips are curved into a warm smile all for me. I will do anything to keep that look of happiness on her face and resign myself to keeping her busy and preoccupied with some semblance of normalcy throughout the day.

SHE IS STYLING her hair as I finish showering after an evening of lovemaking and the sound of the penthouse elevator alerts us to Matt's arrival. I dry off quickly and pull on a pair of lounge pants giving her a kiss. "Get dressed, Sweetheart, we have company," I say, heading out to meet Matt as he walks off the elevator.

Matt walks in and he's freshly showered and changed since last night, but looks tired. "Thank God you're back. I was worried about you," Jenny says, walking into the room in yoga pants and a hoodie.

He gives her a wry smile and smirks. "I'm fine, but the other guys don't look so good. I could use some coffee," he says and Jenny heads to the counter to start the brewer.

"What did you find out?" I ask, hoping that he has something new for me that hasn't already been relayed from him to Jay and from Jay to Scottie.

"We've got a fucking mess that's what. The guys that took Jenny are old world boys. They're out for Mancini's head."

I nod. "Yeah, Scottie filled me in on some of it," I say, gesturing to the dining room table before pulling out a chair for Jenny and sliding into the one next to her.

Leave her to get right to the point. "What do I have to do with it?" she asks.

Matt looks at me and I nod, but not in time. "I was the one that asked the question Matt," Jenny says, but then looks at me, those deep green eyes questioning.

Yeah, now she's catching on. I will control everything that has any potential to hurt her and she's agreed to this but she's battling this internally and has no fucking clue how hot she is when she's pissed. I can't help but smirk as I give Matt a nod to share what he's learned.

"The Chicago family thinks you're laundering money for Mancini and they're going to cut him off at the knees. They thought you were an in to finding out some of his suppliers and distribution networks," he says, pouring himself a cup of coffee from the carafe that Jenny's placed on the table.

"What the hell!" she says.

"They don't know that Ty was laundering the money without your knowledge, but somehow they know his money was floating through your company."

"Chase and Jay took care of all of that. Do you remember the night that everything happened? The night you first came to my house? While you were with me Kate said that Jay and his team were cleaning all the files and getting rid of all the evidence that Ty had been using to launder his dirty money through Torzial," she says.

"Yeah, I know all the details, Jenny. The thing is," he says, pausing and glancing at me.

"Matt, what is it? This is my life we're dealing with. I'm at risk for losing everything and you know how much Torzial means to me," she says.

I hate that she has to deal with this shit and she won't in the future, but right now she needs to know what's going on. I give Matt a chin nod and try to repress my instinct to smirk at the scowl she tries to suppress.

"Jay's team did wipe all the stuff off your computer, scoured your books and got rid of everything that could have led the police to your doorstep. I've been doing some investigating of my own," he says, ignoring my raised eyebrow..

"Tell me," Jenny says.

"You're probably going to be pissed, but I can live with it if we get you out of this mess," he says.

"Tell me," she demands, scowling at him. Shit, her anger isn't directed at me for once. I suppress the need to laugh at the surprised look on his face.

"All of the money that filtered through Ty and into your company traces to you knowing about it, signatures, the names on different accounts. You name it and it all ties back to you."

"I don't understand, it was all taken care of."

"It was, that's what we're trying to figure out, but until then we need to get you and Brian to the Prestian or Larussio compound."

"Matt, we're secure here. We have a safe room and she's already used to the ways to get to it," I say.

"It's not as easy as that, Brian. The Chicago mafia is nothing to fuck around with. If I get you both to the Prestian or Larussio estates it does two things. It tells the Chicago family that if they come after Jenny or you, they're messing with the entire New York family. It's sending a message. It's also going to give the teams a lot more room to maneuver in. A lot more ground that's protected between you and the enemy," he says.

"I get it. I should have bought property in this state, too. The Larussio and Prestian estates have a lot of acreage between the road and them."

"Damn straight! That space allows us to get a lot of people and processes in place between you and whoever is trying to get to you. In all the years that I've worked for Chase we've only sent him to the safe room twice and it's been recent," he says.

"Scottie's been pressing me for years to get an estate in New York and Chicago like the one I have in L.A, but I never had a reason until now. I'll talk to him about it. Matt, how long before you can get us to the Prestian or Larussio estates?" I ask.

"It's a twenty-five minute copter ride in the Augusta to the Prestian estates," he says. I glance down at my cell phone and see an incoming message from Scottie.

Message: Lad we need to talk. Chicago family is after your lovie. Call me.

I need no other warning. "Matt, just got a message from Scottie. He's saying the same thing. Get us the fuck out of here," I say.

"Done, grab any essentials. The chopper's on stand-by. Let's be on the roof in five," Matt says, taking a call on his phone and stepping out of the room so we can't overhear him.

"Leave your stuff Sweetheart, we can have someone take care of what we need," I say, as she begins fussing with papers on the table. She does not protest and in fact gives me that submissive look that makes my dick twitch. Fuck I love taking care of this woman's every need and the fact that she likes it when I do keeps my dick hard. "Grab our coats and I'll get your purse from the bedroom," I say. My briefcase is lying on the chair and I take a moment to slip a couple necessities into it and smirk to myself as I grab her purse and meet her in the foyer. She has our coats and Matt is ready to go.

"There's nothing to worry about. We're well protected," I say as we head into the elevator and up to the rooftop.

"When I give the signal I want you moving towards the helicopter. The men will keep you surrounded, but we need to go fast," Matt says, opening the door to the rooftop. "Let's move," he yells as we cross the short distance to where the sleek grey Prestian Corp Augusta is waiting. One of the security guards starts to help Jenny aboard, but I don't allow it. Instead, I grab her waist and hoist her onboard myself and take the seat next to her.

"Get this thing in the air," Matt shouts over the whir of the blades, closing the door as he jumps into the cab.

She looks pale and scared and I curse the fact that I didn't listen to Scottie and invest in an estate that would ensure her safety and that my property in L.A is so far away. It will be my first priority if we make it through this shit alive. I glance down at the incoming message from Chase marveling in the onboard technology.

Message: Gaby's staying at my dad's place. They're in Europe for the month. She is prepared for your arrival.

Reply: Thanks, Chase. I owe you.

Message: She'll be happy to have company. We'll be at the Larussio's for a while.

My phone rings and I answer it immediately when I see Scottie's picture pop up on the display. "Brian here," I say, as Matt blanches while reading a message on his own phone.

"Listen to me carefully. The mob just hit your penthouse. They want the girl and they know you're involved. We've got crews waiting for your arrival that will get you from the helicopter to the Prestian's. Once you get in the house get in the safe room and don't come out until you hear from me personally," he says.

"Got it!" I say, disconnecting. Matt nods to my phone and begins typing a message. Jenny is looking out the window and completely absorbed in her own thoughts.

Message: Your penthouse got stormed. We barely got out in time. They know the Augusta took off and we've got company in the air. They're about ten minutes behind us.

Reply: What's the plan?

Message: Jay just sent in backup. They'll fly right by us and divert the chopper behind us. It's going to give us a short window of time once we're on the ground. We'll touch down as close to the house as possible and have the security men get you both downstairs.

Jenny's face is pushed against the window. She's been through hell and back and all I want is to protect her.

"Incoming," Matt shouts. "Jenny, Brian, get your heads down. We've got aerial support, but I don't want to take any chances," he yells over the sound of the blades.

I pull her from the window and push her down on the floor

below me, cradling her head in my lap. Her breathing is becoming fast and erratic. "Breathe Sweetheart. Count for me, start with one and I want you to get to twenty. Don't hesitate, do it now," I demand.

"One, two, three, four," she starts, but then pauses.

"Good girl, don't stop until I tell you to," I say.

"Five, six, seven, eight."

"We're clear; they've turned around," Matt yells.

Chapter 15

Jenny

I DON'T KNOW WHEN OR HOW I'VE BECOME THE WOMAN THAT wants a man to take charge, to ensure my safety, and that all my needs are taken care of, but I have. I'm watching out the window when I see lights from another chopper and my body is pulled away from the window. I find myself on the bottom of the aircraft and my face in Brian's lap as his hands caress the back of my neck.

The men in the helicopter are coming after me. I can't control the fear that overtakes me and I can no longer regulate my breathing until his voice cuts through my panic. "Breathe Sweetheart. Count for me, start with one and I want you to get to twenty. Don't hesitate, do it now," he says.

His voice and commands keep me focused. "One, two, three, four," I begin.

"Good girl, don't stop until I tell you to," he says.

"Five, six, seven, eight," I say.

I hear Matt's voice. "We're clear; they've turned around."

"Keep counting," Brian says.

"Nine, ten, eleven, twelve, thirteen, fourteen." The helicopter makes a sharp descent and I quit counting.

Brian whispers in my ear. "Keep counting Sweetheart, otherwise I'll have you recount while I spank your ass." It's all I need to reengage, keep counting and hold my anxiety at bay.

"Getting ready to land," he shouts as the copter descends over the Prestian acres. The helipad is lit up, but the pilot veers closer to the house. He sets down on the lawn and the security team push the door open. "Go, go, go," Matt yells.

We are quickly ushered into the house and to the security elevator. One of the team members enters a passcode that get us into the floor below. Brian's hand is pressing on the small of my back, guiding me forward, down a short hallway that ends at a door. Matt is right behind us and keys in the final passcode.

Gaby, Chase's rotund housekeeper greets us and I throw my arms around her. "Dear Lord, come in. I was so worried about you," she says, giving me a big hug.

"Thanks, Gaby. Chase told me you would help us settle in with Don and Emily out of town. This is Brian Carrington. I think you met at the wedding," I say.

"How could I forget," Brian says, shaking her hand as she leads us into the kitchen area of the estate's lowest level.

"Gaby, I was so glad to hear you would be here," I say.

"They said you may be hungry when you landed so I made a bite to eat," she says, gesturing to the table laden with meat on skewers, crackers, brie, hard cheeses, and other dips and vegetables. "Matt, pour some drinks while I pull out a few other items," she says.

I glance up to see Brian smirking at Matt who does as he's told. It's clear to see who the boss is when Gaby's around.

I take a seat and Matt hands me a glass of white wine. I realize that my hands are shaking when I bring the glass to my lips and almost spill it down my chin. I take a large drink, needing to calm down. I glance over the wine glass that I'm practically inhaling and Brian is watching me intently. His shock blue eyes are riveting and I have a hard time pulling my gaze from them when Matt asks a question.

"Drink, Brian?" Matt asks, pouring himself a coffee.

"Coffee for me too, please," Brian says.

I finish my wine and get up to pour myself another one. I can feel the heat of his gaze boring through me as he watches me over the rim of his cup. I look into his eyes, challenging him not to mess with me tonight. The wine is calming.

"Dammit, not good," Matt says.

"What's going on?" Brian says.

"They've got choppers over the Larussio estate. They're sending a message which means they're aware of the connections between Jenny and the Larussios. They probably don't understand why we're here and not there."

"The accident was all over the news, but no one thinks that Carlos or Karissa will pull out of it thanks to Chase's news update. The public believes they're still in comas with no chance at survival," I say, glancing around. I'm not telling them anything they don't already know. I'm just rambling. I need to calm down.

Gaby puts a fresh carafe of coffee on the table for the men and sets the bottle of wine on the table. "Help yourself dear, it will relax you," she says, unaware of the look in Brian's eyes.

I lift my own at him in challenge and pour myself a glass, listening while they talk. Brian takes a call on his cell from Scottie and every once in a while I see a nod of his head; otherwise he gives no indication of the conversation. "Keep me posted," he says before disconnecting.

"Scottie?" I ask.

"Yeah, he's on his way. He's been in the United States more

the last couple weeks than he has in the last five years." He hits the speakerphone button on his phone and places it on the table.

"Chase here."

"This is Brian. We're in your dad's safe room and I've got Jenny and Matt with me. You're on speakerphone. I just got off the phone with Scottie. Shit's about to go down, man."

"Give me a second, Brian. Let me get Jay connected with us. He's with a team upstairs," he says.

"Sounds good," Brian says, taking a pull from his coffee.

"Brian, I've got Jay and Katarina with me. Go ahead," Chase says a few moments later.

"Just talked to Scottie. Appears a large quantity of product was lifted from one of the dealers on the mafia's payroll. They like Mancini for it but he's went underground and no one knows where he is," Brian says.

"I understand why the police are after me but why everyone else?" I say, taking a sip of my wine.

Chapter 16

Brian

I LOOK AT MATT. IF ANYONE'S GOING TO GIVE HER BAD NEWS it's going to be me. "Sweetheart, your ex was in up to his neck with the mafia. You know he was laundering money through your company, but he was doing that and much more for a lot of people. He was selling information to anyone that would buy it and they don't know that you weren't part of it. They're looking to find out whatever they can to see how far the leak goes. They want to make sure no one can trace the laundering that was going on at Torzial to them now that he's dead, but they also want to learn who else was laundering money through your company."

"Why do they think I knew anything about it? How did they even know about me and Torzial? Matt, you said they got rid of all the evidence that Torzial had anything to do with it, right?" she says.

"You're correct, Jenny. The team erased everything that was on the servers and on the hard drive at the time," he says, but something in his eyes shifts and damn if she doesn't see it.

"Tell me why they're targeting me now then. He hasn't had

access to my accounts since that night and everything was wiped. How did they learn about it?" she says. Her back is ramrod straight, her face is demanding and I have a difficult time not focusing on her little tits that are hard as nails and protruding through the thin material of her hoodie.

Matt knows more than he's sharing. I see it now. It's evident in the way he looks from Jenny to me. I look at Matt and nod. Whatever he knows she needs to be aware of. "Jenny, they're coming after you because documentation exists that Mancini's money, meaning the cash he embezzled from the Chicago mafia, was laundered through Torzial both before and after Ty's death. There's also an email that Scottie learned about between you and Mancini. The police apparently have it, but they haven't divulged it or submitted it as evidence yet which leads us to believe that they have someone working the inside," Matt says.

She's too smart for her own good and catches on fast. "A dirty cop?"

"Yep, that's what we're thinking. Until Ty died they would have just thought he was doing the laundering, but the entries since the rape and after his demise make it appear that you are personally laundering money for Mancini which makes you the most wanted woman on their list right now," he says.

Fuck! She's gone white as a ghost. "Matt, I didn't email with Mancini. I don't know what the email says, but it's not mine." She rests her forehead on her hands and then looks up. "The day he was at my apartment and tried to rape me again. He told me he was in the middle of planting evidence that would put me behind bars. I never thought anything more about it though," she says, telling Matt the same thing she's shared with me, emptying her third glass of wine.

She raises her eyebrows at me as she pours a fourth glass. She clearly didn't learn last time. She's going to take a sip of that wine and knows that I'm going to punish her.

"You need to tell me exactly what he said," Matt says to her.

"It wasn't much. He didn't break into my apartment to rape me. He was there to load stuff on my computer, but said I interrupted him and he wanted to have a do-over with me so he was going to kill two birds with one stone," she says and the emotion and fear swirling around in those big green eyes slay me.

"Fuck, he was trying to cover his ass back then and throw the heat from him to you and that makes sense. We've got people working on trying to trace any hacks on the IP address right now," Matt says.

Jenny is still unusually pale and she thinks the wine will numb her problems. She's toying with her glass, trying to decide. Take the fucking sip, Sweetheart. I'll spank your ass so hard you won't be able to think about anything else.

Her cotton candy lips hover over the rim, teasing me, her tongue peeks out and then she takes the sip, glancing up at me over the glass and from beneath her dark eyelashes. She's too fucking hot for her own good, but she's clearly misjudged my commitment.

"Matt, we'll give you some time to get things sorted out. In the meantime, if you'll excuse us we have some things to work out of our own," I say, sliding my chair back and reaching for Jenny, lifting her over my shoulder.

"Brian, put me down," she protests, but she can't control her laughter. She loves this as much as I do, but she won't be laughing for long. I ignore Matt's smirk and Gaby's reddened cheeks as I cart her like a caveman down the long hall that will lead us to the other side of the house and to the suite we'll be staying in.

I close the bedroom door behind us with my foot. "I think bad girls get their little asses spanked," I say, laying her on the bed, leaving her watching me as I shrug out of my clothes. I know damn well she could get up and march right out the door but she won't. Her eyes are glazed and her breathing has changed and that glow on her cheeks tells me that I'll find a wet little pussy before I even start.

"We can't do that here," she says.

"Nobody will hear you. It's too far away- undress for me," I say.

She's adorable when she pouts and I know she's contemplating her feelings while she slips the top over her head. Those hard nipples of hers are straining against the white lacy material of her bra. She reaches behind and unfastens it and then slowly begins to slide the straps off her shoulders. I know she's deliberately teasing me, but I allow it, enjoying her show. My cock throbs as she pulls the dainty looking lace over her perfectly pink nipples.

"Now your bottoms and panties, quickly," I say, impatient to see her laid out in front of me. She does as I ask. After a day filled with drama she just needs to let someone else take the reins and help her find a needed release. I slide a paddle out of my briefcase and her lips turn up in a smile, making me glad I slipped a couple toys in before we left. Her eyes really widen when I pull out the gag. She didn't think I was serious. She has so much to learn. She's watching me and her breathing has quickened. Her eyes drop to my rock hard cock and when her tongue touches her bottom lip my dick twitches in response. Fuck she's hot.

I smirk to myself; if she wants to come tonight she'll have to beg with a sore ass. I stride to the side of the bed. "This is to ensure your screams don't reach anyone's ears but mine. Now be a good girl and open your mouth," I say, watching her eyes and her breathing carefully. I know this is new for her and I want to make sure we don't cross any emotional triggers for her.

She eyes the ring gag that I have in my hand. I used to like ball gags, but I love the fucking way she moans. While I want to stifle her screams, I still want to hear her little sounds and whimpers when I fuck her later. "You won't be able to talk with this in place." I put a small round ball in her hand. "If you need me to stop, for any reason, if you're at the point emotionally or physically where you need to safe word, you squeeze the ball and I will stop immediately," I say.

She nods. I need to hear you, Sweetheart. Words," I remind.

"I understand," she says.

"You still wanna play?"

"You know I do," she says and she's right. I do know, because I can smell her fucking arousal from here and it's taking everything that I have not to lay her back on the bed and slide into her velvety softness.

"Good. This ring is going to keep your lips from coming together so you won't be able to talk or scream, but I'll still be able to hear you moan. Open those beautiful lips of yours, Sweetheart," I say and she does it without hesitation. My cock throbs like it's the first time I've been with a woman.

I place the ring in her mouth and then fasten the purple suede strap that leads from the rings around her face to the back of her neck. Her fuck-me green eyes are causing my balls to ache and all I want to do is slide my cock in that ring and feel the warmth of her throat around it, but I don't. Instead, I pick her up and with one shift sit on the bed and have her lying over my lap. She wiggles into place and I can't help but smile.

I shift her long dark hair over her shoulder so I can run my forefinger from the base of her neck down the length of her delectable spine. She tenses and goose bumps form on her arms as I let my fingers run over the place where her ass cheeks come together. She tenses and I can feel the inhale and exhale of her chest against my thigh. I spread her legs slightly, inhaling her scent before straddling a leg on top of the back of her thighs. I feel her tense beneath me and her breathing hitches.

I've shown her the paddle, she knows its coming, but I want to feel the warmth of her ass beneath my bare hand first. "This time we're going to count to twenty and when we finish you're not going to want to ever have more than three glasses of wine," I say.

She shifts underneath me and I can't stop my dick from throbbing against the heat of her belly. I bring my hand down hard. "One," she mumbles through the gag and I continue. She squirms a bit, settling into the strokes against her ass, counting along with me until we hit six. At seven she moans and I can smell her arousal wafting up to my nostrils. I inhale deeply and my hand lands on the same place it just was causing the reaction I was waiting for. She moans and grinds against my thigh and my dick twitches. Three more succinctly to her ass ensure that she is completely aroused and panting.

She is right on the edge, exactly where I want her before the first slap of the paddle lands on her ass. I pause slightly, waiting for her reaction. She rubs her little puss against my leg and that's all I need. I bring the paddle down again and my cock throbs listening to her little moans beneath me. I can barely handle the wait, but need to make the next eight mean something. I bring it down again and she squirms, her skin is heated and I intentionally lay the next one on the opposite cheek and alternate. Her skin is reddening nicely and the smell of her arousal barely allows me to finish, but there are stakes involved and I want her to know the difference between fun spankings and punishment and I make sure the last few make an impact.

She pulls away and I pause before sixteen waiting to see if she'll squeeze the ball. She doesn't, but instead lifts her perky little ass in the air as a challenge. Fuck me; I bring the paddle down hard, once and then twice, three times and four before flipping her around to straddle my wrapped cock.

I pull her down onto it and unclasp the back of her gag. She fucking starts to purr as I pull her down, driving with intention, hitting that special spot that makes her scream and come and she fucking does.

"Brian!"

Her pussy is clenching, holding me in place, milking me for all I'm worth and I can't help wondering what she would feel like without the damn barrier, the one I've never had sex without. One night stands, no trust in my partners to ensure a child was not born as a result.

The thought of intimacy on that level with this woman makes my dick spasm, but I hold off my release, needing to steal one more orgasm from her, hear her squeal just one more time and I drive in harder, suckling her neck, marking her as my own until she starts to pant and I can feel her start to tremble around me again. The sound of her sweet little purrs and the feel of her pussy clenching brings me over the edge and I unload everything that I have into her.

I find her lips as we let the waves settle and explore the velvety depths of her mouth with my tongue. The depths of my feelings for this woman is something I've never experienced and I know that I will spend the entire Carrington fortune if I have to defending her and keeping her safe and protected from anyone that is a danger to her, including herself.

Chapter 17

Jenny

I AM STRADDLED ON TOP OF HIM AND HE IS STILL HARD, twitching inside of me and my hands are wrapped around his neck. The worries of the day are gone and all I can concentrate on is his tongue exploring the depths of my mouth, engaging my tongue in a slow dance and his hands stroking my naked back as we come back to earth. I feel cleansed of the worry that was plaguing me earlier and all I can think of is how to let him know how much he means to me.

"You take all of my worries and absolutely disintegrate them," I say, nuzzling into his neck.

"Even when I spank your ass?" he says.

"Especially then. I love that you care so much about my health and well-being that you spank me. Not that it's that large of a deterrent," I say.

"Oh, yeah. Maybe next time you won't be able to sit down for a week," he says.

I know he won't hurt me, but I pretend to pout. "Maybe that's what I want?" I tease.

His hands slide down my waist and run along my sides, caressing my hips, settling on my cheeks. "If you disobey me again you'll find out just how serious I am about your well-being."

I glance up and he is watching me as he pushes the hair that has fallen over my face behind my ear and kisses me. "We should probably jump in the shower and get back to the team. I'd like to hear if they have any updates," he says.

I sigh, content to stay in bed while he heads to the shower. When he returns wrapped only in a towel around his waist, his body is still glistening with water drops and I have a hard time taking my eyes off the dark patch that extends past his towel. His eyes rise and he smirks as I walk by him and head into the shower. When I return he is pulling something out of his briefcase. "Drop your towel and lay down on the bed, face down," he says.

I flip over without question and he pushes my hair off of my back and begins to massage my neck and shoulders. I moan softly as his hands find the knotted muscles and begin to work them into a relaxed state. I think I could stay this way all day, but then he massages down my length and when he reaches my ass cheeks, I feel a cool cream drizzled over my heated skin. He begins rubbing it in and the coolness feels good. "There, now you can get dressed again," he says.

"Why thank you," I say, slipping into my clothes and running a brush through my hair.

He raises an eyebrow at me. "Naughty so soon?" he says.

"Maybe if I'm really lippy you'll put that gag back in my mouth. I've seen pictures of what it's intended for," I say, relishing in the way his eyes light up.

He spins me around from the mirror and lifts my chin so I'm looking into his eyes. "The next time you act so sassy I'm going to gag that little mouth of yours and shove my cock right through that opening," he says, capturing my lips with his own.

I am breathless and wet again when he finishes our kiss. "Let's go get an update before I take you back to bed," he says, opening the door of our bedroom and guiding me down the hall.

We walk through the living room and Matt is listening to Jay over the cell phone at the dining room table. He is nodding. "Jay, Brian and Jenny just joined us. Thanks for the update. I'll give you a call back a little later," he says, disconnecting.

"Jay's team just confirmed that your IP address was clearly hacked. That's the way they got into your email and made it appear you were corresponding with Mancini. While Ty may have initially started this it's clear someone else has taken over those efforts," Matt says.

"Fuck! When did you find that out?" Brian asks.

"Just a few minutes ago. I'm sure Jay's team is preparing some summary for Scottie as we speak and you'll get the word officially shortly," Matt says.

Brian nods knowing that Scottie was relying heavily on Jay's intel team. "This is fucking unbelievable," he says.

Matt takes a sip of his coffee. "Clearly whoever Ty was working with is now working with someone else, it's not the Chicago family and I don't think it's Mancini," he says.

Brian nods agreeing with his assessment. "What's the plan, Matt?" he asks.

"I'm going to infiltrate the Chicago family," he says.

I narrow my eyes at him and stand up. "That's the stupidest idea I've ever heard. You are not going to put your life in jeopardy."

"Jenny there's a lot you don't know about me. I used to run with this group and I know how to get back in," he says.

I try to comprehend what he's said. "I don't care. There's no way that you're going to put yourself in danger," I say.

"It's the only way, Jenny. I'll take a lot of heat for leaving the organization, but I've got a cover story. They may want to kill me when it's over for what I did to their two men, but they'll want me alive until I deliver Mancini to them," he says.

I cringe at what he's said. I don't want to know what he did to those men to make them talk, but I know he did it to protect me. "Find a different way," I say.

"I wish there was, but there's not and too much is at stake. I need to prove you didn't kill Ty and convince the Chicago family that you and Mancini have no connection and that you're being framed," he says.

"I don't understand why you think you're going to learn anything this way," I say.

I look up and barely catch a glance from Matt to Brian. "What is it that you're not telling me? You owe me this much," I say.

At first he just looks at me like he's not going to say a word. He glances from me to Brian and then back to me. "We've been waiting for the letter between you and Mancini to show up as evidence, but it doesn't. We can't figure out what reason someone could have for not wanting that connection made if they're trying to frame you. Jay's intel team has had taps on a few of the police officers that were part of the investigation and were able to trace several of their communications to a well-known member of the Chicago family. We're missing something and I need to go in and get it figured out," Matt says.

I look from him to Brian. "Does Jay know you're considering this?" Brian asks.

"He's the only one that will know other than the two of you," Matt says.

Jay's got a few men coming over that will take my place here at the estate. Keith has been stateside for a while and helped us get her extracted. You may have already met him," Matt says to me.

"I might have. Chase has so many security guards, it's hard to be sure, but I remember Kate talking about him. Didn't he and his wife have a baby not too long ago?" I ask.

"Yep, that's the one. He's a good man and Chase trusts him. He'll make sure that everything goes smooth. Chase and Kate are tucked in at the Larussio estates with Sheldon and his team and Jay has the hospital unit that Carlos and Karissa are on locked down tight, no one will get close to them," Matt says.

"The other thing, under no circumstances are either of you to mention this to either Chase or Kate. The chances of someone catching word on the communication lines could cost me or all of us our lives. Not a fucking word to anyone. Jay will take care of things in the event things go south," he says.

Brian nods. "What's the plan then, when are you leaving?"

"I'll be gone when you wake up," he says.

I can't help but tear up. "Matt, there has to be a different way," I say.

"If I figure it out between now and the time I leave I'll let you know. For now, that's the plan and you make damn sure you pay attention to your security detail. One slip and they could snatch you and this time we may not be able to get you back," he says.

I can't stand it one minute longer and burst into tears and go to him, embracing him into a large hug. "You're like the big brother I always wanted," I say, pulling him close to me.

He hugs me briefly and clears his throat. "I've gotta call Jay. Brian and Keith will take good care of you as long as you pay attention," he says gruffly.

Chapter 18

Brian

I CAN'T HELP BUT SEE THE TENDERNESS IN HIS EYES AS HE settles her away from him. She's told me that he's like a brother to her. He means the world to her and what he's proposing sounds risky at best and I don't want her to lose someone she cares so much about.

"Matt, you're going to have to give me something that makes me believe that's a good idea instead of a suicide mission," I say, looking at Jenny's pale face and those wide green eyes that are so filled with dread.

Matt looks at me and then turns to her before he speaks. "It's the only way. No one else will be able to get the information we need. I'll find out who specifically has it out for Jenny," he says.

"Chase and I have more money than we know what to do with. You need to tell me why you think it's a good idea to go in by yourself and why there's not another way to deal with this," I say.

His eyes cloud over and he looks between me and Jenny. "There's a history here Brian, just leave it alone and let me do what I do best," he says.

"Jay and Chase know about your history?" I say, more for Jenny's benefit because I already know.

"They do... Chase and Jay saved my fucking life. There's nothing I wouldn't do for them. The only way to protect Jenny and keep it from coming any closer to Chase and Jay's doorstep is to drop off the grid and go back in," he says, taking a pull of his coffee.

"Let me pull Scottie in. He thinks that the Larussio head of security was dirty, took Kate's parents out and is in bed with Carlos's brothers and uncle, meaning the Italian mafia."

"He might be right Brian, but no one gets pulled in. I need to disappear quickly and if he knows he may interfere when it's critical that he doesn't. Unfortunately Brian, you're right in the middle of this. They think Jenny's still laundering for Mancini and I'm sure they have the extraction on camera which is exactly why I wanted you to stay put while I went in for her."

She narrows her eyes. "Don't look at me like that, Sweetheart. I wasn't about to let Matt have all the fun," I say.

"Matt, the minute you disappear Chase will have Jay pull in every resource it takes to locate you. I don't know why we don't tell him what's going on and let him provide you with the support you need," I say.

"Brian, you're not hearing me," Matt says and I glance up at the tone in his voice.

"I'm fucking listening. What aren't you telling me?" I say.

"I can't trust the teams. A lot of fucking people are dirty," he says.

"You mean other than the people that hit the Larussios?"

He shakes his head and looks over his coffee cup at me. "I don't fucking know yet. I need the Chicago family to think I'm trying to get dirt on Mancini and that we didn't know he was working for them," Matt says, taking a swig of coffee contemplating this.

It's clear he's going in whether I like it or not. "I need to know the plan, to support you," I say, seeing the look of fear in Jenny's eyes.

"Mancini was connected with Ty and the laundering of money into the Torzial accounts. Ty comes up dead; Jenny is accused of murder and then kidnapped. We go after her thinking it was Mancini that snatched her. If I play them back the tape it will confirm we didn't know it was the Chicago family that we were dealing with. After the way I left their men they're gonna want a little pay back, but I'll deal with it," Matt says and I watch Jenny visibly blanch.

The stubborn fucker still isn't listening. There's no fucking way that I'm letting someone that means so much to Jenny jump into a fucking hornet's nest without protection. "Two things are going to happen. You're going to tell Scottie everything that you know and he's going to work with you to develop a plan to get in and then get you the hell out of there safely," I say.

"Brian, no disrespect man, but I can't put our lives in the hands of someone I don't know," he says.

I contemplate this for a moment. "I can completely understand your hesitancy, but what you need to understand is that Scottie has been with my family for years and dedicated to both me and the Carrington enterprises for years."

"I get that Brian, but it's a relationship thing. I don't know him, how he works, and that's critical for this type of mission. I've contacted a few of my old partners and we've got it covered. In the meantime, there are a couple things that you both need to know. Lets' go over them now," he says.

I can feel my jaw clenching watching the pulse in Jenny's neck beat and realize that talking to this stubborn fuck about his suicide mission is getting us nowhere fast. I'll deal with it after he's gone.

"I will never give your name to anyone. If someone tells you that they have me and will let me go if you give them something or tell them something, they're fishing or they have me and there's nothing you can do to change what happens. Do nothing, they're trying to draw you out at that point," Matt says, kissing the top of her hair and reaching over to shake hands with me.

"He knows what's he's doing, Sweetheart," I say, after he's gone, internally contemplating how to fix this.

She nods. I wait for her to say something, anything, but all I get is the trembling of her bottom lip. I've read the reports about her real brother. I also know she's come to rely on Matt and all I want to do right now is wipe every bit of uncertainty or doubt that he'll return from her lovely face.

"He'll be okay, Sweetheart. I'll do everything within my control to make sure that he is," I say, caressing her cheek and wiping the tears from her eyes.

"Thank you for all that you tried to do. He's so stubborn. I hate that he's putting himself in danger because of me," she says.

"He loves you and wants to take care of his baby sister," I say, kissing her forehead and pushing the long strand of dark hair out of her eyes.

"He's been the closest thing to a brother to me that I've had in years and he's been by my side through the worst ordeal I've ever experienced and now he's gone, putting his life in jeopardy," she says.

I lift her chin so I can see her eyes. "Why don't you go get some sleep, I have a little more work to do," I say, kissing her lips and watching her walk away before I begin sending out a text to Jay.

Message: We need a plan in case things go south for Matt.

Reply: Give me a minute and I'll give you a call.

There's no fucking way I'm going to sit idle while he puts his life in jeopardy. Jenny would never get over the guilt if something happened to him while he was trying to help her.

The phone rings and I answer it immediately. "Jay here," he says.

"Matt told me and Jenny about his plan to head back in. He seems confident, but we both know this could go south real quick."

"Yes, it could, but make no mistake Brian, Matt is well aware of the risks and don't doubt his capabilities for one moment. If he didn't have a well-thought-out plan and mitigation strategies for things that could go wrong he wouldn't be going."

"I still don't like it, anything could go wrong," I say.

"You're right, and that's what I was working on before you called. Here's the deal. An old running buddy of mine is on the inside right now. I can't say too much more than that, but we've been in contact. He'll keep a watch out for him and do what he can if things get too hot, but it's gonna cost and Matt doesn't need to know," he says.

"Money isn't an issue. Tell me what you need and how you want it processed and it will be done."

"I appreciate that Brian but with what Chase pays me I can cover it. I wouldn't feel right about using the Prestian account since he didn't want Chase involved in any way."

"He's going in for Jenny. It's on my dime. Send me the instructions and make sure it's not traceable," I say.

"Will do, Brian," Jay says before disconnecting and I immediately hit Larry's contact to get plans in place for the arraignment coming up.

Chapter 19

Jenny

IT'S BARELY FIVE A.M. AND HIS SIDE IS ALREADY EMPTY. Today is the day, and I have thought of nothing else all night and every night for the last few weeks. I slide into a silky, peach-colored robe that is hanging in the bathroom and grimace at the length, barely hitting the tops of my thighs. I walk into the kitchen, glancing around to make sure no one else is around before finding Brian at the table talking on his phone.

I put a K-Cup in the machine and can feel the heat of his eyes watching me while it's simmering.

"Fuck! Do whatever it takes to get this resolved," he says, disconnecting and flipping the phone onto the table.

"Who and what was that about?" His blue eyes are like a window of cracked glass and it's hard to discern the emotion passing over them. "Brian, if this is about me, I should know," I say gently, slipping into his lap and kissing him firmly on the lips.

It takes him a moment, but then he nods his agreement. "It was Larry. My attorneys and his detectives are doing everything within their power to find out who really did this, but time is short, just a few weeks left and they're not any closer yet," he says, hugging me tight.

He has spent the last three weeks trying to convince me that we should put off court proceedings as far into the future as we can but I am convinced that right will conquer wrong and that the court will see that I could not possibly have been a part of something so heinous even though before it happened there's nothing that would have made me happier than to see Ty dead.

The last few weeks awaiting the arraignment have been the most excruciating. I know he wants to help, but he's done everything that he can. I have world class attorneys and they have prepared me well during this time. I try to muster the cool as a cucumber look that Kate says I have when dealing with project negotiations. The one where outwardly people think I'm not rattled by their subtly implied hints of using another company if the price isn't lowered while inside I'm worried sick over the potential loss.

"Justice will prevail, it always does, it has to," I say, kissing his lips and sliding off his lap to pour myself a cup of coffee, unwilling to look into his eyes. "I should go get ready for the show," I say, turning and heading to our bedroom.

———

OUR SECURITY HAS DONE a great job getting us to the courthouse without incident and we have just gotten out of the car and are halfway to the front doors when a voice rings out, "Jenny Torzial!" I scan the area looking for the voice, and see a man walking towards us with a mic in his hand trying unsuccessfully to get through the wall of security Brian has placed around me.

"Jenny Torzial we understand you are being accused of murdering the man who beat and raped you. Do you think that gives a woman the right to act as judge and jury and take another human's life," he says as people turn and start to gather, listening to the spectacle.

The security men have him blocked and Brian's hold on me tightens and his pace quickens, but I come to a complete halt leaving him no choice but to follow suit. I don't know how they know this or what has come over me but in that one moment, those two questions strike a chord, a willingness to fight back, not only for myself, but for all the women who have found themselves in similar situations.

Brian's arms tighten around me, guiding me away from the throng that has gathered. "Ignore it," he says, but the interaction has left a myriad of questions floating through my mind and I can still hear the reporters shouting questions in the crowd, but security has us surrounded and they can't get through.

As soon as we enter the courthouse Brian guides me into a small recessed alcove, no more than a little waiting area which is currently unoccupied. He pulls me into his arms and forces my chin up so that I'm looking into his eyes.

"You're trembling, Sweetheart," he says, removing his long black wool coat and placing it around my shoulders, over my own jacket for added warmth.

Larry walks into the room wearing a grey dress suit with a black tie and white shirt. He looks even more intimidating today than he has sitting across from me at the dining room table, drilling me and I am relieved that he's on my side and not that of the prosecution. "Time for the show, kids," he says.

"Thanks, Larry, we'll be right behind you," Brian says, extending his hand to his attorney before he heads to the courtroom.

He takes my waist and pulls me close to him. "Look at me Jenny. It will be okay, answer the questions they ask, just like we've gone over. Don't be afraid. You know you didn't do this and Larry and his team are first class defense attorneys. Chin up, head back and back straight. You have nothing to feel guilty about, nothing to feel remorseful about or to be afraid of. Understand? If you get nervous, focus on me when you're talking, just like only the two of us are having a conversation," he says, kissing my lips lightly.

My heart is swirling with so many emotions right now that I can only nod my understanding, but thankful that this strong dominant man has been placed in my life.

"Come on, time to go," he says, placing his arm around me and guiding me into the courtroom.

Chapter 20

Brian

AS WE WALK INTO THE COURT I SCAN THE ROOM TAKING IN the witness stand and the desk where the court reporter with bright red lipstick sits, waiting as we file in and take our seats. The court- room is relatively empty and I take a seat directly behind Jenny and Larry and the cadre of attorneys I have hired for her and glance at the other side of the room.

The plaintiff's attorneys, in this case the state council, are just getting situated and talking among themselves. They aren't the run of the mill state attorneys. They are the top gun contracted guys they bring out for these sorts of cases. They have an air of confidence, talking with each other as though we're invisible. Chase and Kate walk in a few minutes later and he slides in beside me placing his arm around his wife as she takes a seat next to him.

"What are you doing here? She didn't want either of you to be drug into this," I say quietly glancing around and taking in the security strategically placed around the room.

"There's no way we were letting either of you go through this alone," Chase says, raising his eyebrows at me.

"Thanks, Chase," I say.

"Will the people in the court please rise?" A white-haired judge walks out of a door dressed in the traditional long black robe. He proceeds to the tall, old-worldly looking bench presiding over the court. "Please be seated."

The arraignment information is reviewed by the court and both attorneys have an opportunity to provide additional details and information that support their case. She is called to the stand and walks with her head held high and back straight and is sworn under oath before she is allowed to be seated. They finally get to the question about innocence and guilt and her eyes drop and she is chewing her lip, a behavior I've come to know well. "Ms. Torzial, we will repeat the question if necessary."

She looks up and the deep dark green of her eyes capture mine. "That won't be necessary. I plead not guilty," she says and I slowly release the breath I didn't realize I was holding until that very second. "I plead not guilty to murdering the monster who beat and raped me repeatedly until I was unconscious, but that wasn't enough for the asshole. He wanted me to remember every sordid detail so he forced me to wake up and then started all over again."

"Objection," the prosecution yells but that doesn't stop her, nor does the judge's gavel coming down with a thud and a yelled "sustained." "Ladies and gentlemen when I found out Ty Channing was dead I did rejoice, my only regret is that I wasn't able to kill the fucker myself," she says over the continued objection of the prosecution.

My heart swells with pride but I know it wasn't easy for her. I follow the lines of her neck and can see the gentle swell of her chest raising and lowering. I catch her eyes with my own. Deep breathes, Sweetheart. The shuffling of people moving around pulls me back to the matter at hand and I nod to Larry who is already been hauled up to the judge's bench along with the prosecution. I know he will be the one to bear the brunt of getting her out of a contempt of court but I also know any price they set except for jail time can be managed with a quick exchange of a monetary signature. It is more than twenty minutes later when the court is openly addressed.

"Please rise," the bailiff says. Larry has already warned me of the anticipated outcome, but here I am holding my breath desperately hoping that he's wrong. All of my fucking money and influence comes down to this. Everyone stands and I can feel the tension emanating from Jenny from where I sit behind her and it kills me not to be able to take her in my arms and protect her.

"We believe there is probable cause and sufficient evidence to try the defendant Jennifer Ann Torzial for the crime of murder in the first degree as charged. We will schedule a preliminary hearing in two weeks. Court is adjourned."

Larry prepared me for the fact that in all likelihood the court would move forward with charges. Jenny is not a flight risk, until now has been viewed as a fine upstanding member of the community, owns a company that contributes to the community tax base, has a family that depends on her and has no priors to speak of, which made getting bail for her after the arrest as easy as signing over a quarter of a million dollars.

What I'm not prepared for is the date for the next hearing which is set for two fucking weeks away. The proceedings adjourn and I put my arms around her slumped shoulders as I guide her out of the courtroom. "I'm so fucking proud of you for telling your side of the story," I say, kissing her lips tenderly.

"I don't know what came over me, but I had to get it out. All the paparazzi swarming around me, knowing all of those questions will be fired at me over and over in the next few weeks. It just got to be too much," she says.

"Young lady, you've just completely flipped our entire strategy, and while I'm not excited about the ass chewing I just took, I want you to know that what you did took courage. We're going to fight this and come out winning, but you need to be prepared for the long haul. It's going to take time but we're going to prove that you did not do this," Larry says as we near a ladies room sign.

"Thanks, Larry. I'm really sorry that I got you into trouble with the judge. I need to stop by the restroom," she says to me.

"I know you told me this could happen and most probably would, but I want your teams working on her case round the clock. You tell me what you need to get an innocent verdict and it's yours," I say to Larry while we wait for Jenny.

"We're doing everything that we can. They should have allowed us to throw the journal out and it should have never been used even as a reference today," he says.

"Do you think you can get it removed eventually?"

"Possibly, but probably not. The one thing we have going for us now is that she's come clean about the rape. We can take a different angle. We need to focus on a new strategy," Larry says.

"Hey, didn't think I'd catch up with you," Scottie says, walking up to us and shaking hands with my attorney.

"Nice to see you again, Scottie," Larry says.

"I know this is going to be difficult to hear lad after the hearing, but there's something I need to share with you about your lovey. We just found multiple emails and files on her hard drive and you're not going to like what they contained any more than I like being the one that has to share it with you," he says.

"What the fuck? Tell us," I say, knowing that my attorney needs to know everything that he has to say in order to defend her.

"Brian, I know this is going to be hard to digest, but..."

"Spit it out," I say, cutting him off with no patience.

"You told me that Jenny didn't know who you were when you met her at the Prestian wedding?" Scottie says.

"I did, and she didn't. I mean she knew my name, because we worked on the Prestian Corp project over email, but only as the COO of Prestian Corp, not as Brian Carrington," I say.

"Yeah, well it would appear that she knew exactly who you were. We found an email chain between her and her friend talking about you and the plan to meet the elusive Brian Carrington, sole owner of Carrington Steel Enterprises."

"What are you saying?" I say, knowing what I heard but not processing.

"We found an email between her and her friend dated way before you met. She knew exactly who you were and was trying to develop a plan to meet you long before the night of Chase and Kate's wedding."

I feel like someone just punched me in the gut. I try to comprehend what he's saying, put it into some fucking perspective, but every woman that's been after me and my family's fortune for years is swirling around in my head right now. My mother staying with my father, not out of love, but for his money- not caring that he was making out with half the town, right in front of her fucking nose. Anything to keep the money, and the women that would do anything to please me, do what I told them, just for a chance at bagging one of the richest men in the world. I hear him talking, but can't process a fucking thing he's saying for a minute.

"Are you hearing me, Brian?" he says and I try to pull myself out of the free fall and concentrate.

"I'm listening," I say, trying to get my head back in the game.

"I know you care about this girl, but you can't keep kidding yourself lad. All the evidence points to her guilt and if you're not careful she is not only going to snag your money, but will drag you into one of the biggest mafia wars this country has ever seen,"

Scottie says and all eyes are on me waiting for some sort of response, but what's swirling in my mind right now needs further contemplation.

"Well we definitely wouldn't want that. You should listen to your security advisor and attorney. We wouldn't want the elusive Brian Carrington to get snared by a little gold digger, especially one that kills off all of her exes. Who knows, you might be next," Jenny says, stepping out from the wall around the bathroom.

I start to say something, but the coldness in her eyes stops me dead in my tracks. Her deep green eyes have turned as hard as jade and she walks past all three of us and strides right down the long corridor away from us.

Larry is still talking and I try to focus on what just happened. "We need time to talk about the strategy going forward. I've had people reaching out to all the newscasters who captured her story trying to buy the footage, but we won't know until morning who took the offer and who didn't. It's a crap shoot right now. We need time to develop a different strategy with the information we have, unless of course you want to wash your hands of the entire mess," he says.

I look from him to Scottie before glancing down to read the text from Keith outlining Jenny's intentions. She doesn't know it, but she might just be safer at her own apartment if what's racing through my mind is true. Fuck! We all glance up at the figure turning the corner and waiting inside the doors of the front exit. "I need to take Jenny home. We'll talk later," I tell Scottie and head for the door, placing my arm around the back of her coat before we head outside the courthouse doors. I fill my lungs with the cold crisp air, trying my best to stave off the waves of nausea that threaten to overtake me.

We get into the back of the limousine and Wes navigates us through the congested Chicago traffic. I don't know how long we've been driving before he eventually pulls up to the Carrington sky-rise against security's objections. The doors of the limo are opened for us and we are immediately surrounded by security teams attempting to hold the paparazzi at bay behind the red ropes that encompass the walkway into the building. "Just keep your head down," I say, ignoring all the questions thrown out by the news crews as we make our way toward the private elevator that will take us to my penthouse and out of the ensuing chaos that exists around us.

"Thanks for your help," I say, making sure all the internal cameras are off before the young security officer sheepishly takes off Jenny's full length coat and winter hat.

"Anytime, I'm going to head down to the security office before anyone else returns. Oh, and boss, don't worry. The teams will keep her safe until everything gets sorted," he says, before leaving me with my thoughts.I shrug out of my suit jacket and loosen my tie, throwing it onto the dining room chair before pouring myself a finger of the finest scotch money can buy, and looking out over the vast city of Chicago from my penthouse in the sky.

I play the scenario in my mind again and again, and my heart knows the answer even though my brain is having a hard time processing it.

Chapter 21

Jenny

My mind is swirling as I head down the long courtroom hall wanting nothing more than to get away from this place as quickly as possible, but it's not safe. I send a message to Keith asking him to meet me inside the doors of the south side exit and as I turn the corner to head down the hall that will take me there, I see him arriving.

"I'm glad you texted me."

"I want to go home but I need security," I say.

"We need to get you somewhere that affords you more protection than your apartment."

"They'll come after me at those places because they know I was moved from my apartment and assume I won't go back. Disguise someone and put them in the car with Brian. It will appear as though I'm going back to wherever he's going with him," I say, shrugging out of my winter coat and hat and giving them to him.

"Brian's going to want you to return home with him," he says, shaking his head.

"They can wear these, and you need to get me something to change into and smuggle me back into my apartment. I can work from there, won't cause you any grief and you can put as many security men in place as necessary. I have savings and will pay for the time of the men and before you say anything else, I am not going home with him," I say.

The clenching of his jaw belies his irritation but he texts a message to someone. "The teams will get everything in place. They'll need about ten minutes," he says to me.

I GLANCE at my computer calendar. I don't know what I thought, but after two weeks maybe that he would call or reach out by text and apologize? I don't expect him to believe me over his head of security, hell, the entire world and court is choosing to believe what they hear, but after what we've shared, just something?

The last couple weeks have been an excruciating reminder of how painful trusting someone with your heart can be. The only thing that has kept me sane while confined to the apartment is working diligently with his attorney team via Skype, going over question and answer sessions a gazillion times until I am dreaming of nothing else, and it is a relief that my day in court has finally arrived.

I prepare myself for the event, slipping into a mid-calf tan and black wool skirt, black boots, and a silky tan cami with a black jacket layered over the top of it. I cringe at the big puffy blonde wig that I will wear to go to the car, just in case anyone is watching the apartment.

I do not relish the call to my mom. As much as she wanted to be here, she has enough on her plate and I'm happy that I was able to talk her out of coming. There is no way that I want her to have the memory of seeing her daughter in court being charged with something so heinous. It will be hard enough for her and my family to deal with the news once it spreads. I make the call and it is another half an hour before I am able to disconnect, my heart breaking as I make out the slight sobs that she is trying to prevent me from hearing on the other end of the phone.

I look down and see the first message from Brian that I've had in two weeks. He has a car waiting outside for me. How fucking noble. I ignore it and instead send a message to Kate who is waiting with Chase and his security team downstairs to take me to the courthouse where the last hearing of the day will be mine.

We walk into the courtroom and I see Brian's shock black head of hair. He is sitting in the pew a few steps away from me and I avoid his eyes and those of the man sitting next to him, the man who has condemned me without a shred of credible evidence. We stop and Kate hugs me one last time before she and Chase take a seat next to Brian. I walk with Larry the rest of the way, two seats up where I will be seated for the duration of the court session.

I can feel the heat of his presence and his gaze following me as if he was sitting right behind me and not two rows away. I've barely taken a seat when the bailiff issues the "All Rise," order. I stand back up and take a good look around at the court. The bailiff is a tall skinny man with short brown hair dressed in dark navy blue pants and a light blue uniform shirt, the court reporter is the same short spiky dark haired one from my arraignment and she's sporting the same outrageous bright red lipstick.

I wait with bated breath as the white-haired judge walks into the courtroom and he is as intimidating as he was the first time. My legs feel like they are going to give out underneath me at any time and it is a relief when we are finally allowed to take a seat. The judge begins reviewing the details of the case for the court and before he has even finished, if I were a juror I would presume me guilty of all the awful things they are accusing me of.

I only hear bits and pieces of the arguments and the information that is provided from the prosecution and defense. The words battered girlfriend, rape victim, deviant sexual tendencies, and mafia ties are just some of those echoing in my head.

In a mere matter of an hour the decision that will impact the rest of my life is made and the court is convened. I know before the judge says a word that I will be tried, I've thought about nothing else for weeks and prepared for it, so when it's shared with the court it's not a surprise. It was my own decision not to plea bargain for a crime I did not commit but no amount of honesty or truth telling was going to get through to a court that had already condemned me to a trial before I even walked into the room.

I've felt it coming for weeks. Walking in and seeing Brian and Scottie sitting in the courtroom together after what transpired and having the judge confirm it in words only solidifies my anger and feelings of injustice. I tune out most of the formalities and focus on my breathing, watching all of the court proceedings play out in front of me.

My attorney shakes hands with several gentlemen in the room before guiding me out of the courtroom, attempting to shield me as best he can until Chase and Kate join us with their security team.

Brian's security guards are outside as I exit the courthouse, doing their best to keep the onslaught of news reporters and flashing cameras at bay, but he is nowhere in sight. He may not want to have his name associated with me any longer, but I do appreciate him keeping his attorney on the case and ensuring security is in place until this is all over.

Kate and I slip into the back seat of the limo and Chase settles in across from us. It is only a little after five in the evening, but the sun sets early in the blustery winter nights of Chicago. The city lights are growing brighter as night encroaches and we make our way across town in the busy rush hour traffic. They seem to know I need the quiet, but Kate's hand rubbing my shoulders is comforting.

I keep replaying the information from today in my mind. That damn journal. Everything kept coming back to that and in the end it is what sealed the decision to move forward to a trial for murder in the first degree. No amount of money Brian had could keep it from being submitted as evidence and time and time again it referenced my desire to kill Ty. It's not a lie that I wanted him dead and when he attacked me for the second time if I had killed him instead of breaking his nose it would have been deemed self-defense, but I didn't and it wasn't.

The driver navigates the city, circling and talking with other teams to ensure we are not being followed before heading to the back entrance of my condo. "It's not over yet, Jenny," Kate says, embracing me in a long hug before helping me into the wig. I can't talk or I will turn into a sobbing mess so I just nod and allow the security team to surround me and lead me through the back entrance and up the stairs.

"Thanks for all your help and for staying with me the last couple weeks," I say to Keith who comes into the condo and sweeps it one more time, before taking his position outside of my door.

All I want to do now that I'm home is to strip out of my clothes and slide into a warm bubble bath, drink a glass of wine or a few bottles and put all the pieces of my life together. I have barely begun to undress when the text arrives.

Message: I'm coming to pick you up.

Nothing has changed and I don't know how to get past the fact that Brian's own security team thinks that I killed Ty. I keep replaying Scottie's conversation over and over in my head and Brian didn't say one thing, not one damn thing in my defense.

I know I shouldn't, but in a short time I will be going to trial for murder and if today is any inclination of the verdict than we should clear the air between us. I think about it for all of two minutes before I slip out of my court clothes, rummage through the options in the closet, quickly pick out a pair of jeans, a shirt and my new boots before rereading Brian's text and messaging a response.

Reply: Yes.

I pour a glass of wine to settle my nerves, take a long sip and then read his response on my phone.

Disguise myself? What the hell.

Chapter 22

Brian

It's been almost two fucking weeks since we've been in the same room together except for the hearing today and I can't get the woman out of my mind. My cock twitches and my balls contract just thinking about seeing her again. I know it's not a good idea yet and that I should have waited, but her one word response sends my ass into action. I send a text to Paulie.

Message: Just received a note the penthouse may be under attack tonight.

Reply: WTF?

Message: Put the penthouse on lockdown. Official word is I'm going to bed early.

Reply: Anything you say boss. We'll have it covered.

Message: Everyone but you. I need you to pick me up in five minutes. Make sure we're not followed and send Vitrie to get Jenny in the silver cadi. Side entrance. Fill you in later.

I look at myself in the mirror and shrug out of my suit and slide

143

into a pair of jeans and white t-shirt, and grab a jacket and baseball cap out of the closet before texting Jenny.

Message: Disguise yourself. Go down the main elevators to the third floor, and then down the stairs and the side exit of your building. Vitrie will be waiting in a silver car. I'll meet you when it's safe.

I slide into the back seat of the limo that is waiting as I arrive downstairs. "Thanks, Paulie," I say.

"No problem. You gonna tell me what's going on? I just put my ass on the line with all that penthouse is under watch bullshit," he says.

"Soon, just drive. Head north and tell me when she gets picked up. We'll have to double back and make sure no one is following her," I say.

"Who the hell is making sure we don't have a tail?" he says, looking at me in the rearview mirror.

"Sorry Paulie, but I can't trust anyone but you and Vitrie right now."

"Fuck, you say that and I'm about to be sick."

"I can't be sure yet."

"Vitrie just picked her up," he says, slowing to take a glance at his phone.

"Excellent, have him head towards us and then let's make sure we don't have a tail before we circle behind them," I say.

"We wind around the city for at least a half an hour before Paulie is comfortable that we're not being tailed and then double back entering the highway a good distance behind Vitrie and Jenny. Paulie is watchful and has Vitrie make a few lane changes and exits to ensure no one is being followed before he gives them directions to a place just off the highway and down a side street. He slows and pulls up next to the silver Cadillac.

I start to get out, but he stops me. "No, I'll get the girl," he says, slamming his door as he walks over to the car.

He looks around and it's then that I notice his hand on his belt. In that one instant I don't fucking know who to trust and I scramble out of the limo door just as she's getting out of the car. Paulie takes her by the hand and at the same time shots ring out. "Get down," he yells, throwing himself over the top of Jenny before I reach her on the ground.

Shots ring out again and I push her farther into the earth, trying to cover every part of her uncovered body with my own. "Fireworks, its' fucking fireworks," Vitrie shouts.

"Mother fucker," Paulie yells, scrambling to his feet as I pull Jenny off the ground and into my arms.

She's standing there looking shell shocked with tears running down her face. "Thank you," she says, trying hard to wipe the tears but they're coming faster than she can manage.

It's at that fucking moment with Paulie looking like the jackass of all times that I know he would give his life for either of us and that I can trust him completely.

I reach out and shake his hand. "You're a good man, Paulie. You were right when you said something got bent with my parent's detail, and the same thing happened with Carlos and Karissa Larussio. We have a traitor or two in our midst and we can't be too careful," I say to him before Vitrie joins us.

"Vitrie, play tail for a while until I give you the say so," Paulie says, as he approaches.

I watch as she dusts herself off and retrieves the wig and hat that have fallen off her head. She's dressed in slim fitting jeans, boots that ride up to her knees with a little bit of lace peeking out over their tops, a lace cami under a see through blouse and her dark brunette hair is mussed and flowing in ringlets past her chest.

I slide into the back seat and pull her into the car with me as

Paulie slams the door and her eyes are wide eyed green pools, questioning, looking for answers and I can't take my eyes off her. She's like the fucking life water I've needed to quench this dying feeling inside for the last two weeks.

"I've only ever seen you in jeans and a t-shirt once before," she says quietly, and I can't tell from her expression if she's pleased or just making conversation.

I laugh. "Really, well, you look lovely, too," I say, smirking.

"When did you come back to Chicago? I thought Kate said you were spending most of your time in New York," she says.

"Yeah, I was there working for the last couple weeks," I say.

"I see," she says, but she doesn't sound like she believes me and that rubs me the wrong way after the crappy two weeks I've had.

"I've been working on the Carrington expansions and your defense and you know I live in multiple cities. I call home wherever I need to be at the moment," I say.

She shrugs and looks out the window.

Fuck, when she agreed to meet me I saw this little reunion playing out way differently. She's still clearly pissed and I can't blame her. She has every reason not to trust me after she overheard Scottie's accusations and I didn't defend her. "I didn't intend to fight with you tonight. I know what a horrible day it's been for you," I say.

She nods and I take that moment to pull her closer. Her deep green eyes search mine and she bites her lip. "We both know that I have very little time left and when you sent me that text I thought it would be a good opportunity to clear the air. You're a good man Brian and I don't blame you for not believing me, hell, the courts don't even believe me," she says.

I start to interrupt, but she keeps right on talking like she didn't even hear me.

"I don't know how to defend myself anymore. They have my

journal and everything in it is true. I wanted to kill him and when he attacked me the second time I tried and didn't succeed. They think I plotted out his death and went on a hunt and killed him. As much money as you have and as many lawyers as you've thrown at this you can't change how this looks. If I were sitting on a jury I would probably find me guilty and that's exactly what I expect the outcome to be," she says.

It's obvious that she's all but given up and I find that un-fuck-ing-acceptable.

"Paulie, book a hotel suite and drop us off," I say, watching Jenny for a reaction. The lowered eyes and change in her breathing is all the indication I need.

Paulie drives around for a short time and then pulls the limo up to the most exclusive hotel in Chicago and we get out. "You'll be in the Larussio penthouse under the name of Mr. and Mrs. Moretti. The rooms are paid for."

"I didn't want the Larussios involved in this," I say.

"They don't have a clue. Jay gave me a key card to this room for a weekend when I did him a solid," he says as we pull up to the front of the entrance.

"Thanks, Paulie. Ready, Mrs. Moretti?" I ask, assisting her out of the limo as the valet opens the door.

She hesitates for a moment, but I know the lusty desire swirling in those deep green eyes. I hold out my hand and let her contemplate and she grasps it in her own. The suite is every bit as luxurious as I would expect at this hotel. The city lights and water taxis making their way up and down the river can be seen from the window, but the only view I want is standing right in front of me with the widest green eyes and they mirror my own lusty need.

I take her in my arms crushing my lips against her and she opens for me, letting me explore her sweetness while I hastily undress her. I want to feel every inch of her against my own skin. I feel like a man that has been denied air and water for two fucking weeks. When she is naked I scoop her into my arms and take her to the bathroom, letting her slide down the length of me and let my hardness rub against her lower belly. I feel her tremble when she feels it. I turn on the shower and hastily peel out of my clothing, leaving it in a heap on the floor as I guide her under the water. I push the dispenser, filling my hand with the vanilla scented body wash and warm it in my hands before turning her against the wall and massaging it into her neck, kneading her shoulders and rubbing my hands and the scented moisture down the length of her spine to that delectable little ass in front of me. My cock is hard and firmly pressed against the crack of her ass, but I want her to know this is more than sex for me and turn her around to face me, kissing her gently while soaping the length of her creamy neck, along her collarbone and down the swell of her breasts, swirling each nipple as I go.

I kneel in front of her and want my hands wrapped around her hips, so I grab them, pulling her closer allowing me to inhale the scent of fresh soap and the uniqueness of her pussy. It's like an aphrodisiac. Her eyes are glazed over with excitement and I know she feels the connection, the chemistry and love we have for each other.

I tease her for as long as I can before letting my tongue wash over her sweetness. She is already on the edge, her hands pushed against the shower walls to steady herself, but I want our bodies joined as one and quickly wrap before sliding into her heat in one move, not wanting her to ever forget the experience of our bodies together and the trembling of her climax tightening around me, the wetness of her desire and when I tell her to come that's exactly what she does.

As soon as she nuzzled into my chest and found my heartbeat she was fast asleep. I've barely closed my eyes all night watching her. I finally resolve to getting something done and head into the kitchenette, put a pot of coffee on to brew, turn my phone back on and flip open the Mac. I glance through all the messages from security sending me updates on the supposed penthouse issue. No evidence of foul play was found, fancy that.

I send an email to Larry and tell him to push the trial date as far into the future as he can. I want her free for as long as possible to give the teams and Matt time to figure everything out, but his response is immediate letting me know that it has to be Jenny's decision.

I spend the next couple hours rereading all the reports, one after another in the off chance that we've missed something.

She walks into the kitchen and my breath catches. She has my t-shirt from the night before on and the shadow of her firm little tits and perky nipples are all I can concentrate on. I lower my eyes from her breasts with difficulty and her French tipped toes remind me of the first time we were ever together. The reality that I may lose her in a matter of weeks hits me like a brick, but I need to be strong for her sake.

"Hungry? I ask.

"Ravenous. I think someone took all of my energy," she says, smiling at me with those cotton candy colored lips of hers, selecting fruit and a croissant from the tray in front of her.

"Would you like some coffee?" I ask, pouring myself another cup.

"That would be great," she says, lifting her mug for me to fill and taking the New York Times from the tray and flipping through its pages while she sips her coffee.

I close my laptop and try to decide how I want to approach the conversation that we need to have. I let her get half way done with her breakfast before I broach the subject. "I'd like to explain some changes to your defense strategy and why I didn't defend you or call you until yesterday," I say.

She looks up at me with those wide green eyes and all I can see is a sea of swirling emotion. "Brian, after yesterday all I wanted was to feel you in my arms again, at least one more time, because after the trial I don't think I'll ever have that chance again. I don't regret it and will always remember it, but let's face it, your entire team thinks that I'm guilty and so do you."

I start to refute it, but she raises her hand to stop me. "I'm not done. I don't want or need your charity. What I needed was your trust and you had every chance in the world to defend me and didn't and now I know exactly why. Why don't you go back to your girlfriend and stay the fuck away from me," she says, heaving the entire bulk of the New York Times newspaper across the table before walking back into the bedroom and slamming the door behind her.

Chapter 23

Jenny

I **WAKE IN A STATE OF SEXUAL** HAZE, SORE AND SATED, AND start realizing that Brian's not with me. I look around the room and check my phone for the time. I send Keith, the security guard that Chase has standing in for Matt, a note to let him know that I'm okay and will let him know the plans for the day a little later. It's just past six a.m. and my belly is growling from all of our exertions the night before.

I slip into his t-shirt that is still lying across the armchair and pull it over me. He's so tall that it covers me decently. I wash up, brush my teeth and head into the kitchen to find him.

He's working on his computer, but has an enormous breakfast spread lain out in front of us and I am absolutely ravenous. I know we should talk at some point, but for now I'm just content with the fact that we spent a blissful night together in each other's arms and even though he didn't stick up for me he still seems to care for me.

I snag a croissant and begin taking a few bites while he pours me a cup of coffee before flipping open the Times to look at it while he's finishing up on his computer. I skip the front page and slip back to the social page trying to steer clear of the court headlines. The picture of him and the blonde Russian ballerina posing for the camera at the children's fundraiser is splashed all over the page from the night before last. "Carrington Industries and Sasha Enterprises team up to raise over ten million dollars for the disabled children's effort." His hand is around her waist and she's pulled tight against him and her eyes are fucking devouring him.

It's all I can do to calm the rage as he talks about a plan for my defense. Why the fuck does he even pretend to care? He starts to say something else and I can't even listen anymore. I unleash, calm and controlled. I know what the fuck I feel and right now it's nothing more than severe disappointment that not only has he not defended me to his team, but that he's still clearly in a relationship with someone else. So much for not doing relationships! I slam the bedroom door behind me. I strip out of his t-shirt wanting it off my skin and gather my clothes up and head into the bathroom.

"Jenny, open the door. I'm not sure what you think but let me explain," he says.

"Fuck you," I say barely above a whisper. I'll be damned if he ever knows how much he's hurt me. At least when you're abused or raped you know what it is, pure hate and evil, they don't give a fuck about you, they want to hurt you. But when you think someone really cares about you this time and they betray your trust after getting you to expose your weaknesses and desires it's a whole different story.

I finish dressing and the rapping gets louder. "If you don't open this door I'm going to bust it down," Brian says.

I text Keith that I will need a ride home asap along with the hotel name before I swing the door open and look into the blue eyes staring at me intently. "You helped me find myself after Ty.

You helped me open up, taught me to trust again, exposed me to emotions and desires that I didn't even understand and all so you could discard me and hurt me? Stay away from me," I say, pushing past him and heading out the door to the elevator, riding it downstairs just as a sleek limo pulls up to the entrance and Keith and his security team guide me into the back seat.

The driver navigates the car into the congested city traffic. "How did you get here so fast?" I ask.

"I've been here all night. I get paid to make sure I know where and what you're up to at all times. It's the only way to keep you safe," he says.

He must have been following us all over the city last night. "Thanks, Keith," I say.

"Why all the secrecy about where you were?" he says, as we pull up to the back entrance to my condo and the rest of the security team surround us as we go inside and make our way to my floor.

"Let's just say that I don't exactly trust everyone on the Prestian Corp payroll after all that happened. I trust you because Matt told me to and that's the only reason," I say, low enough so only he can hear.

"Fair enough, but if you trusted me then you should have told me what you wanted to do. I would have gotten you there safe, end of story, no fucking drama."

He's right and I know it, but I also didn't want the fact that I went to see Brian getting back to Chase because then it would get to Kate and then it would be a thing. I don't know how I thought it wouldn't get back to them. "Sorry Keith. I know babysitting me isn't exactly the greatest job in the world."

"Got that right," he says, swiping the keycard to my condo door after we get out of the elevator.

"I'll let the guys know things are back to normal. Next time you want to leave the complex you let me know or we're going to have issues," he says, taking a walk throughout the apartment. Everyone knows that anytime I come home they are to ensure no one has gotten into my apartment because of what happened with Ty and they don't know how much I appreciate the gesture even if I don't vocalize it.

"I take it you'll be staying in tonight?" he says, watching for a reply.

"I'm in for the night," I say, before he leaves. The only good thing about the last month is that it forced me to get past my fear of sleeping and being alone, safe in the protection of the guards outside my door and to see my counselor routinely.

It is later in the evening after a hot shower and glass of wine before I power on my phone. Ten missed phone calls and text message after text message from Brian wanting to explain. A picture is worth a thousand words. I delete the messages without listening to the voicemails; whatever he has to say at this point is of no relevance. I was doing fine on my own the last couple weeks. Okay, so maybe that's not really true as I think back to the days I stayed in bed crying instead of getting up, but towards the end it did force me to figure it out, stand up on my own and do some good for my business. That's what putting sixteen hour days into the company every day will get you.

I pull open my laptop to start working on a plan to get the last of the expansions for Torzial Consulting moving toward implementation. Once complete I have to resign myself to the tough stuff. The court decision was not in my favor and the evidence against me is pretty overwhelming. If I go to prison I need a plan to ensure that Torzial will continue and that it continues to support my mother and nieces and nephew. This is what I need to focus on.

I pull out the documentation that the attorney and I went over before the arraignment. When it came right down to it the most damning information was my journal. That provided them with the motive, a rape, and written documentation that I, Jenny Torzial, dreamed of snuffing the fucking life out of the bastard and when they ask me in court I will not lie, I will tell the fucking truth.

Chapter 24

Brian

SHE'S GONE AGAIN AND I TOSS THE FUCKING NEWSPAPER INTO the fireplace. What the fuck did I expect her to think? I send her a message and resign myself to give her a little to cool off before I reach out to her again and text Paulie to pick me up and take me home. On the drive home, I set up a time to review her case with Larry later in the day and once settled into my office begin going over the documents he's prepared, but there's nothing here except the report that Scottie put together for me.

OCCURRENCES IN ORDER:

- Twenty million is transferred from four major pharmaceuticals into one off shore account that can be traced back to Ty.
- Chase Prestian and Katarina Meilers meet with Ty Channing and Jenny Torzial at Torzial. Camera

footage shows they were escorted by 4 guards including Jay himself.

- Chase and Katarina leave Jenny's office and go to the Prestian towers condo in Chicago.
- There is footage of Ty and Jenny leaving the Torzial floor and getting into his car.
- Approximately forty-five minutes later Ty's bank transfers are frozen and reversed. (See detail page 45).
- Approximately three hours later Katarina is taken via limo to Jenny's condo. We have intel that suggests Prestian Corp men were surrounding the building keeping surveillance while she was inside.
- Two hours later, more of Prestian Corp security detail was deployed to the condo, and Katarina was escorted by limo and Prestian security back to his condo in Chicago.
- An hour later, police officers respond to alarms at Ty's office downtime.
- Ten minutes later Ty leaves his condo and twenty minutes later arrives at his office. Reports are filed.
- Five minutes after Ty leaves his condo the security system is tripped, but appears to have been scrambled. It never made it to the police station.
- The next day, Torzial is hit with a subpoena for documents related to pharmaceutical accounts and a drug laundering charge. (See details appendix 2 page 11).
- Ty is admitted to the hospital beaten to within an inch of his life, sodomized and left with broken bones and a Larussio mafia symbol that he'll have for life.
- Jenny begins counseling. Appointments are scheduled twice a week and were arranged by Chase's personal

assistant. She seldom goes and never stays the full hour.

- Jenny Torzial's accounts are cleared involving the drug laundering case two weeks later.
- Ty is released from the hospital and three days later accepts a job with one of the major corporations representing one of the largest pharmaceutical companies in the globe in LA.

IT IS mid-morning before I finish, having read the document in entirety several times along with every one of Scottie's updates. I've always known Chase's family was close to the Larussios, but nothing mafia-like has ever come across my desk before. I slam the document down, everything for the last two weeks is pointing to the same thing and I feel it but don't have a shred of proof, yet.

I hit Jenny's contact and the call still goes right to fucking voicemail. I'll give her until the end of the day, but that's all the patience she'll get from me.

I hear Celia letting Larry in for our meeting. "I didn't know you intended to come in person," I say, standing up to shake his hand as he walks into the kitchen.

"What I have to say needs to be done in person, no phones, no wires, no cameras. I need your assurance Brian, my license or life could be on the line."

What the fuck. "You can be assured that I have no wires or taps on you or me, but the sky-rise is set up with cameras. My security team will already know that you're here and the film will have captured you to this point. You give me the word and I'll have them turn this room off," I say.

He turns pale. "They can see me but you're sure they can't hear me?" he asks.

"Correct, keep facing me so they can't read your lips. My team is multi-talented."

"Then I'm going to give you an envelope and be on my way. I trust that you'll destroy the contents after reading it. Find a meeting spot that we won't be recognized in and come alone. The details and reason are in the envelope. No security team, no cameras, mics, nothing," he says, handing me an envelope before turning and walking towards the door.

I open the envelope and read the contents and for the second time today send documents swirling into the fireplace. Fuck me! I hit Paulie's contact, the only man I know on my team I can trust, but I don't fucking know who's monitoring his calls and immediately think better of it. After what Larry just gave me it confirmed my suspicions and I can't fucking trust anyone.

Message: Looks like what they're saying about Jenny is true. Can you and a crew pick me up around front? I need a little wind therapy.

I head into the bedroom and don my gear. It's been three fucking months too long since I've felt the hum of my Harley underneath me. I grab my helmet and head downstairs and one of the guards pulls up on my bike. "Nice ride, Boss," he says.

"I need one of you to follow me and three of you to head to Jenny's. I don't know what the fuck is going on, but no one lets that little cunt out of your sight, got it? She makes one move out of her apartment and I want to know about it," I say.

"Got it," Paulie says, giving orders to his crew as I throw my leg over my bike.

"Vitrie, you're coming with us," Paulie says, not even giving me a chance to tell him I need him alone. We pull into the city traffic with Vitrie in the front, me in the middle and with Paulie bringing up the rear until we hit the highway and veer north. We ride until Vitrie accelerates up the highway and Paulie pulls alongside me motioning that I should follow him before he accelerates. I throttle back the gas and stay on his ass until he signals right and leads us into a deserted road. He brakes right in front of me, gets off his bike and heads back to me signaling me quiet with a finger over his mouth.

He shows me his cell phone before motioning me to the edge of the water dam. He sets it on the ground and then motions me to follow him away down the trail and deeper into the woods. We reach the clearance and a waterfall comes into view. "You have about five fucking minutes before someone realizes we're not in a dead zone and they've been made. What gives?" he says.

"I don't know who to trust right now."

"Yes you do or you wouldn't have called me instead of Scottie," he says.

"You know when you said that something got bent years ago with my dad's death? Was it him? My dad trusted him with our lives."

He looks at me for a few seconds before nodding. "It's possible," he says after a short pause.

"I need you to give me something here Paulie," I say.

"I've suspected for years, but didn't and still don't have one bit of proof. I've spent all this time trying to stay close to him, keeping my ears to the ground. All of a sudden your girl comes onto the scene and we've got Scottie showing up and on the waves chattering to the Italian mob," he says.

"The fuck, Paulie?" I say.

"I wish to fuck I knew what the motive was back then and what it is today, but you can bet your ass your father's death wasn't an accident and we need to find out why it happened and what connection it has to your girlie," he says.

"Can we trust Vitrie?" I ask.

"We trust no one which is why I had him come with us. If I hadn't brought him it would look suspicious, but we need to hurry. I sent him around the ridge to scope things out, completely plausible to keep you safe. If we get separated the story is you stopped at the waterfall and just did a little self-reflecting. Got it?

We need to get our shit and circle back with him and get someone we trust to your girlie's apartment. Your little act with Larry and calling her a cunt was a good ploy to keep whoever it is that's after her guessing, but we can't be too careful. We're dealing with mafia, embezzlement, and fucking enforcers stealing from the mafia and running it through your girlie's hands. If I were them I'd want her out of the picture so she's not squawking in court."

The only other people I trust with Matt gone is Chase and Jay. I send a message to them both and then send her a message once I read Jay's reply.

"Let's get to her condo fast and by the way I need you to set up a private meeting," I say.

"Larry?"

"How do you fucking know that?"

"He was your father's attorney and ever since you cozied up with your lady friend Scottie's had our team detailing him hard," Paulie says.

"Fuck, so you already knew before I even told you?" I ask.

"Let's just say I was pretty fucking suspicious but the moment you tossed the envelope from Larry into the fire and called me with that bullshit message I knew shit was about to get real."

Chapter 25

Jenny

If I go to prison for the murder of Ty, a life sentence is likely and there will be no possibility of me living out my father's legacy. I was prepared for the court decision not to be in my favor but the amount of evidence against me is overwhelming. I pull open my laptop and begin to make a few modifications to the work I previously started. These changes will ensure Torzial Consulting will become a great enterprise one day with the ability to support our family into the distant future. In less than an hour I've done all that I can do. I have no doubt that Kate will keep the company on its feet and profitable, which will allow the trust to continue sending money to my mom and family each month. There is nothing left to do, but get through the trial and accept the outcome.

It is late evening before I begin reviewing the finalized plans, the outline and execution plan and send Kate a text.

Message: You have a few minutes?

Reply: Of course. Call me when you want.

I hit FaceTime just needing to see my best friend's face. She

Via Mari

and Chase are sitting up against the headboard of their bed.

"Hey, if you're busy we can talk tomorrow," I say.

"Nonsense. What's on your mind? Pretty sure if you call me this late that something's pretty important," she says, moving the camera so I can only see her.

"Can Chase still see and hear me?" I ask.

"What's going on? He's always willing to help."

"I know, and I don't mean to seem unappreciative but I'm at a dead end. You were both in court yesterday and can draw your own conclusions, but if I were a betting girl, I'd put odds on the jury sending me to prison."

My cell phone swooshes and I glance down. A message from Brian and I am just about ready to ignore it, but the message captures my attention.

"Security is on its way. DO NOT TRUST THEM!" Stay in your apartment until I text you with an all clear. TRUST ME."

"Kate, Brian just texted. There are people surrounding the apartment. I don't know who to trust. I have to go. I sent you an email in case something happens," I say before disconnecting. I walk to the door quietly and look out the peephole and sure enough, three burly guys that I recognize from Scottie's crew are standing outside of my door. If my daddy taught me anything it is to be prepared. They're not getting into this condo without a fight. I pour a glass of red wine for courage and finish it in two swallows. It will be the only one I drink to ensure I have a clear head if they bust in.

I quietly push the barstools against the door, load them up with dainty crystal wine glasses and then spread olive oil from the door all over the floor before grabbing the largest knife out of the block on the counter. I lock the bedroom door behind me and then do the same once inside of the bathroom.

I take a quick scan of the room and slide the toilet paper off of the bronze colored floor- model holder. It is heavy, weighted at the bottom and I can do some serious damage with this. There are a couple of candles in glass jars that can be used to throw at the perpetrator, but they remind me that the lighter is in the drawer and I grab it and then open the counter below.

Yes, that's exactly what I need. I pull out the chemicals for cleaning, grab them up and ready my lighter. There is no one in the world that can help me right now except for myself, but even still I send a message to Brian and Kate.

Message: Security outside my door. Chairs with glasses and oil placed in front of the door and I am in the bathroom.

I immediately receive a response back from Brian.

Reply: 12 minutes away. Jay will have men there shortly. Stay put.

As pissed as I am right now I know that I can trust him and Chase's head of security, but I also know a ton of shit can happen in that time.

I grab the little stool from the linen closet and place it below the window so I can see outside and immediately feel nauseous. All thoughts of overtaking the men outside my condo who will be knocking down my door soon just flew out the window, as I see more limos pull up and men that Brian employs getting out. I don't know who to trust.

Message: Security is EVERYWHERE.

Reply: I'll be there shortly.

Message: I'm scared.

Reply: You're on audio text. Keep talking Sweetheart.

Message: I had one glass of wine- need a hellava lot more to drown this shit out.

Reply: I'll let you drink another when I get there.

Message: What about your rules?

Reply: They still apply. So far your ass is safe.

I am about to reply when police and firetruck sirens begin to wail in the distance. I watch out the window as the sounds grow nearer and the men jump back into their vehicles and peel away. I send a message to Brian.

Message: Not sure what's going on. Police and firetrucks just pulled up- men are leaving.

Reply: Jay's been busy.

I hear loud banging on the door and then it sounds like the door is crashing in. "Bathroom at the back!"

I hear that and I don't even take the time to reply. As soon as they come through this fucking door I may not get all of them, but I will do them harm. I step onto the little stool underneath the window and do a quick check. The security men that were canvasing the streets are now gone. The police and firemen are outside on the street. It is a long way down, but if I can get out the window there is a wide ledge right underneath it. The voices are coming closer and the only way that I can get to the police is if I can hoist myself up and squeeze through the opening.

I slide the latch to the left and as soon as I do all the sirens downstairs sound pale in comparison to the wales of the alarms the opening of the window sets off. It's not too high, but upper body strength has never been my thing and even with the help of the stool I barely pull myself up, but the adrenaline kicks in and I use every bit of muscle power to get my head and shoulder out of the window before I hear Brian.

"Jenny, let us in, it's all clear," he yells and I breathe a sigh of relief right before a hand is placed over my mouth and captures the back of my head from outside the window.

"Going somewhere?"

Chapter 26

Brian

I TEXT JENNY TO LET HER KNOW THAT THE SECURITY TEAM can't be trusted and put in my Bluetooth speaker. I don't fucking know how we ever got by without voice to text capabilities before, but as I jump on my bike and head toward the highway and accelerate they are a necessity.

I give Vitrie a chin nod when he comes off the ramp and slides in behind us. I hear the beep that indicates an incoming audio message and Siri relays it for me.

Message: Security is EVERYWHERE. I'm in the bathroom.

I reply to her before doing anything else, needing to put her mind at ease as my own is spinning out of fucking control.

Reply: I'll be there shortly. Stay put!

I then send a message to Jay and he responds almost immediately with the plan. I then message Paulie to let him know they've doubled security around Jenny's apartment, men are on the roof, and that Jay is sending the police and ambulance in as a diversion.

Message: I'm scared.

Reply: Jenny, keep texting until we get there.

Message: I had one glass of wine- need a hellava lot more to drown this shit out.

Reply: I'll let you drink another when I get there.

Message: What about your rules?

Even scared to death she tests her boundaries. A good submissive she is not and I wouldn't change a fucking thing about her. Vitrie flies past me, his pipes rumbling as he accelerates and takes the next exit ramp disappearing from my view. I instruct Siri to call Paulie.

"I sent a note to Scottie alerting him to the fact that you met with Larry today and he gave you an envelope with evidence that shows Jenny is guilty. He's going to see the surveillance tape with Larry talking to you and see you tossing the evidence into the fireplace. The message I sent him will align with what he heard you tell the security team about her being guilty. As soon as I sent that message to Scottie, Vitrie let me know that he had to head back to the house and send the last week's surveillance tapes to Scottie. That right there tells me that Scottie may have been using him for information all these years, but Vitrie's not privy to the shit that went down or is going down right now or he wouldn't have told me."

"Thanks, Paulie."

"Don't thank me so soon. There's a reason Scottie didn't send that request directly to me instead of Vitrie. We need to get your girlie into a safe place until we figure this out," he says, making me accelerate my speed.

As we round the corner to Jenny's condo police sirens and ambulances fly by us surrounding the outside of the building. My phone beeps alerting me to Jay's call as I follow Paulie into the back lot.

"The diversion did what it was intended to do, Scottie's security team left the rooftop and the men that were outside her door hightailed it out of there. They'll be back for her though. We have a small window of opportunity, let's get in and out. I've got Keith with me," Jay says just before we reach him.

I follow him, Keith, and Paulie, taking the elevator to the floor two floors below hers, then into the stairwell making our way up the next two floors to her condo. "Jenny, let us in, it's all clear." Jay raps loudly on her door. There's no response and my fucking patience is done. I hit the door with my foot and all the pent up frustration of the day right below the lock. It shatters and I hit it again, busting the door wide open. "Watch the floor! It's covered with oil," I say as we move through the living and dining room. I gesture towards the bedroom door which is closed, and I know she's barricaded this too. Jay and his team get through the bedroom. I stalk toward the bathroom door and pound the door with my knuckles. "Open up, it's me," I say, and when she doesn't I fear the worst and hit it with the power of my foot, caving it in on the first try. I grimace at the inadequacy of this fucking security.

Jay and Paulie fall in behind me and she's half out the window, her ass is in the air, and her legs are hanging from the window. I grab her around the waist trying to pull her down without hurting her, surprised at the ease in which she falls into my arms and the strength that she uses grasping around my neck.

"You came for me," she says, nestling into my chest. I can feel the rapid beating of her heart and I feel like a fucking super hero as she hangs onto me for dear life.

"Of course, Sweetheart," I say, turning her and kissing her lips.

"When did Matt get back?" she says, looking at me like I have a clue what she's talking about.

Matt pops his face through the window above us. "Didn't think you could get rid of me so easily did you? Still trying to keep you from getting yourself into trouble," he says, hoisting himself through the window and jumping to the floor, ruffling her hair while she's still in my arms.

"You two could have told me!" she says, pouting at me.

"I didn't know myself," I say, holding her closer. "Sweetheart, there's a bunch going on that we need to tell you, but if you keep putting that lip out I'm going to give you something to suck on," I whisper into her ear so only she can hear, carrying her into the dining room with Matt following behind.

She is looking at me with those wide green eyes, but she doesn't say a word, just keeps looking at me. I know at some point we're going to need to tell her what's going on, but right now I just want to keep her body pressed next to me and safe in my arms. I move past Jay and Matt and into her kitchen.

Matt and Jay both look around the apartment and nod to the door and it takes a minute but not that fucking long to realize they think the place is bugged. "I don't care what the fuck you assholes have to say it can all wait until we get the little bitch back to my place and she explains why she's been embezzling millions of dollars from the mob," I say, putting her down and taking her wrist in my hand, walking toward the door and letting them follow me out. I recognize more of Chase and Jay's security men and nod to them as they let us past them and into the elevator.

She's looking up at me and her eyes are wide. If someone is watching through the cameras in the hall, that's exactly the look I want them to capture. We get into the elevator and I know the transmission is shit. "The apartment was bugged, we had to make it seem as though we don't believe you. We'll get you to a safe place," I say, pulling her close and kissing her hair.

"Fucken A," Matt says, immediately beginning to text a message on his cell phone.

The sleek black Lincoln pulls up at the curb as we exit the south side of the building and Matt opens the door so I can slide into the back seat with Jenny. She's still not talking and clinging to me like she did after the assault.

Once in the car Jay and Matt seem to relax, engaging the overhead for a call from Chase. "We've got her and we're heading to your house," Jay says.

"Excellent. Can she talk? Katarina is beside herself with worry," Chase says.

I look at Jenny and she nods. "She'll call her back on a private line, but change of plans, we're heading to my own place," I say, hitting the button to cut off Jay's displeasure and allowing the privacy glass to slide into place.

She's still watching me, her deep green eyes are wide and fearful and I want to relieve any anxiety that she has. "What I said was for the bugs that were planted in your apartment and to give the impression to anyone watching that I was displeased with you," I say.

She's still watching me, but nods. I know it's too soon for her to process everything after what she's been through tonight. "Call Kate," I urge, giving her my secure line.

She nods again and enters her friend's number. "Hi," she says breathlessly. I wonder if she wants to have privacy from me while she's talking to her bestie, but instead she wraps her arm around my waist even tighter like it gives her strength.

"So did you and Brian work everything out?" Kate says and I'm so close that I can hear every word they say.

I feel her arm tighten around me in response. "He would do anything to keep me safe, but it really doesn't change anything," she says, knowing full well that I can hear her side of the conversation. I can't blame her for thinking the worst after the picture of Sasha and me, but I tried to call her and explain, she wouldn't answer, and now she's going to learn to trust me or not the hard way.

Chapter 27

Jenny

WHEN THE DOOR CRASHES IN BEHIND ME I SCREAM, BUT NO one can hear me with Matt's hand over my mouth. "Shh... it's Brian and Jay," Matt says. My heartbeat is racing a million miles a minute, but then I hear Brian's voice and his hands are grabbing me by the waist and pulling me down from the window and into his arms.

He turns me around and his eyes penetrate mine. The emotion emanating from his eyes is mesmerizing and I find myself grasping his neck tighter as he carries me out of the bathroom and after a brief conversation with his team he puts me down and practically drags me toward the elevators.

As soon as Jay and Matt have me settled into the back of the car I know we're going to be safe. He answers his cell phone and is still watching me intently, his gaze heating my skin. We're going back to his place and I don't argue. I believe what he tells me, that he didn't mean the things he said about me being guilty, but the words are still painful to hear. There is so much left unsaid between the two of us right now. He may not be into commitments, but I do know that he will do his very best to keep me safe and protected and for that I am grateful.

"Call Kate," he says, handing me the phone after finishing his conversation with Chase. I know she must be worried sick the way I left the conversation so I use his phone and call.

She answers on the first ring. "God Jenny, I was so worried about you," she says.

I laugh. "I have to admit I was right there with you. I wasn't sure what to expect but I was ready. I had the lighter and some chemicals all set to go. Whoever came through that door was going to get a homemade mace spray," I say.

"What about Brian? You have to admit that was pretty romantic him charging to your rescue," she says. I should have known she would bring him up. Just because she and Chase are happily married and have the storybook ending doesn't mean that Brian and I will. At some point I will tell her about Sasha, but right now the hurt is too deep.

"I know he will protect me, but it really doesn't change anything," I say, turning my head toward the window and lowering my voice. We talk for a bit longer before hanging up and I feel the heat of Brian's gaze penetrating me.

He pulls me close and although the privacy glass separates us from everyone else in the car he whispers in my ear. "You walked out without letting anyone know where the fuck you were going, knowing that you were in danger, then you don't answer any of my phone calls or texts. What kind of punishment do you think that warrants, Jenny?" he asks, pulling me against the heat of his body.

"You lost the right to talk to me like that. I saw you with your arms around the very person you said you weren't in a relationship with. I may be submissive as you put it, but I am not a doormat and Keith and the team picked me up. They knew where I was," I say.

His grip tightens and his hand steadies beneath my chin

turning me toward him. "I was honest with you, but you didn't give me a chance to explain the article. Instead you thought the worst and stomped out like a spoiled child and put yourself, my team, and Chase's in a great deal of danger."

"I saw the picture Brian. You had your arm around her and it was clear from the look on her face that she was with you," I say, not backing down an inch.

"I had my arm around her as we posed for a picture after the ballet troupe and my company contributed millions of dollars to help needy children. It was a show of solidarity of the combined forces and I've told you before her feelings aren't reciprocated. I'm not used to explaining or repeating myself."

"You really weren't with her?" I ask.

"No, I most definitely was not with her, but you are right that she still wants a personal relationship. I don't, but I'm not going to let that stand in the way of providing funds to kids that need help," he says.

"Alright, then I'm sorry I assumed the worst. I'm not used to relationships and when I saw the picture after you hadn't contacted me for a couple weeks, I guess I thought the worst, that you had gone back to her."

"I have been and will always be honest with you, but you are going to need to learn that, Sweetheart. Being mine means trusting me completely and you've shown me that you don't."

I try to look away and avoid the disappointment in his eyes, but he holds my chin steady. "I want no one else. Now, I'll ask you again, what kind of punishment do you think that warrants?"

I have no control over my body's response, immediately wet and so intensely turned on that I can feel the heat rising in my cheeks and my nipples straining against my shirt. "You decide, whatever you feel is appropriate," I say, catching the audible intake of his breath.

"You have no idea how much that turns me on. I'll show you how much later, but right now I want you to rest. Take a sip of this, it's got a bit of sedative that will help you relax and it's going to be a long trip."

I start to ask questions, but he puts his fingers to my lips. "Shh... rest now. We'll talk later. I have work to do in order to mitigate some of your recklessness," he says, kissing the tip of my nose and shifting me so that I'm lying in his lap.

The adrenaline from the day, coupled with the knowledge that Brian doesn't want that blonde haired vixen allows me to drift peacefully off to sleep. I can vaguely hear him talking and at one point I am hanging onto his neck as he carries me, giving orders to everyone around him, but my mind drifts with exhaustion until I feel him shaking me. "We're home, Sweetheart," he says as I start to wake up and the car door opens.

"Make sure Kate and Chase know she's home and safe. Jay and Matt, give me about a half hour to get her settled and I'll meet you in the study. I need to make sure everything's worn off and she's comfortable," he says, lifting me into his arms.

I put my arms around his neck and hang on, too groggy to protest. He makes his way to the large glass expanse that doubles as a doorway. I'm not sure where we're at, but it's the biggest home if I can call it that that I have ever seen. "Is this your house?" I ask.

"It is, but I don't often spend time here, mostly for socializing with the Hollywood folks when I'm in town," he says.

The contemporary home of white stone and glass looks like a movie star mansion that seems to rise out of the earth with a backdrop of mountains and surrounded by lush green hedges and palm trees in my blurry state. It's just a few short steps to the ornate double door and Matt holds it open while Brian carries me through it to the foyer.

We walk past a long contemporary white marble bar with the

wall behind it taken up by bottles of high end booze, with the longest television monitor I've ever seen above them. Down a very short flight of stairs I see a large competition size pool table and a view of the mountains from the glass that acts as a wall around the room. He heads the other way though, walking into the glass encased elevator and presses the fifth floor.

"You seriously have five floors in this house?" I ask

"Actually more, the lower levels and garage aren't accessible this way," he says, kissing the tip of my nose right before the doors open and he carries me down a large hall, until we reach the double doors at the end. He pushes them open and the suite is encompassed in a wall of clear glass with a magnificent view of palm trees swaying in the breeze.

"Who the hell needs this much space?" I say, nuzzling into the heat of his chest as he walks.

He smiles down at me. "It was an investment after my parents passed away, but serves as a great place to hold parties and you'll be grateful for the space when all the Hollywood elite gather to talk business and have a little fun. It's also the perfect place to learn about some of the things you've dreamed about and desired for so long," he says, carrying me into his bedroom.

I am starting to come out of my grogginess and aware of the hard-muscled firmness of his beating chest as he holds me. "I like the sound of that, but we've done all that stuff, spankings, restraints, even though I don't think you were particularly hard on me," I say.

"Yeah, you've done well. Now we're going to explore your depths of trust, but before we get to that I want to make sure that the sedative your counselor provided has worn off and you don't have any side effects," he says, placing me on a king size bed with an intricate bronze head and footboard. I can see the vastness of the city landscape and the twinkling of the lights as dusk begins to fall. It's like we're looking over the entire valley and we are.

"Where are we?" I ask.

"California, Bel Air," he says.

"You seriously drugged me and flew me halfway across the country? We're really in California?" I say, knowing the answer before he even gives it.

"Your counselor was concerned about your well-being with everything that happened. She recommended a very low dose sedative that relaxed you; otherwise I wouldn't have given it to you. She'll be here to talk with you tomorrow."

"You don't need to fly her across the country to have a session with me. Seriously, we can just talk on the phone," I say.

"She asked to see you today or tomorrow and I wanted to make sure you were in a secure area."

"I thought we were going to Chase and Kate's?"

"That's where Jay wanted to take you, but Alfreita and anyone after the Larussios right now would have thought you were there."

"You pretty much kidnapped me," I say, feigning petulance.

The blue of his eyes flash from light to dark. "Kidnapped you or got you out of a situation that you had no chance of getting out of yourself? We haven't set boundaries yet, so I'm going to let that comment go, but trust me when I tell you that I intend to teach you the true meaning of trust," he says, kissing me not so gently on the lips.

"I said I was sorry. When I saw the picture of the two of you I thought you were a couple and that I wasn't anything more than someone you had a bit of fun with."

"I told you that you were mine and that I love you and even after that you still took off putting yourself and my team in danger. Totally unacceptable."

I nod knowing how difficult it must have been for him to open up to me about his feelings. "I love you, too," I say, reaching up to kiss his lips gently.

"Get freshened up and take a look around while I make a call and get this mess sorted," he says, kissing my lips gently and caressing my cheek before heading toward the door.

"Thank you, Brian," I say, feeling suddenly overwhelmed that he cares so deeply about me that he's carted me off halfway across the country to keep me safe.

"You're welcome. You'll find clothes hanging in the closet and in the dresser. Meet me in the living area when you're done for a drink and don't wear panties," he says, as he closes the door behind him.

Chapter 28

Brian

HER CHEEKS LIGHT UP WITH COLOR AND I CLOSE THE DOOR behind me smirking to myself. After all the anguish she's put me through I want her little pussy to be dripping for me tonight. Matt, Jay and Paulie are downstairs at the bar watching the fight when I join them.

"How big is that screen?" Matt says, tipping back a glass bottle of Coca-Cola.

I shrug. "It's only seventy feet; I had it put into the design knowing I would be entertaining a multitude of different clients and people here in Cali. A large screen is always a good idea to get people collaborating," I say, pouring myself a finger of scotch.

"Gentlemen, Jenny is going to be downstairs within the hour. I presume you have an update Matt?"

"Yeah, but it's fucked up at best," he says, glancing at all of us gathered around the table. It's been three long weeks since he left and I just want to hear what he learned.

"We all know that proving Jenny's innocence is going to be

difficult without blowing the entire fucking mafia world open and having all the families come crashing down on her," he says.

"We do, tell us what you learned?" Jay says.

"I think we all knew Mancini killed Ty or that someone did it and tried to frame him, but what we didn't know were his ties to the Italian Larussio family," Matt says.

"Fucking A, like I told you all of a sudden your girl comes onto the scene and we've got Scottie showing up and on the waves chattering to the Italian mob," Paulie says, looking from me to Matt.

"The fuck guys, what's going on?" I say.

"Your father's death wasn't an accident and we need to find out why it happened and what connection it has to your girlie," he says, nodding to Matt to continue.

"Brian, you're not going to like what I have to say, but I need you to hear me out," Matt says.

I nod, but can feel my pulse race and my entire body tense as I wait for what he has to say.

"What I learned is the staggering amount that Mancini embezzled, millions and millions from the mob and he laundered a great deal of it through Torzial. Ty sold Mancini out to the Chicago mafia and was offed before he could collect what he thought they'd pay him. Stupid fuck thought he was going to get paid on both sides of the fence. Now Mancini is on the run and has reached out to the Italian Larussio family for protection."

"Why would that family protect him?"

"They were more than interested in taking him on board when they learned that Carlos's daughter's best friend was laundering money for him, the same person in charge of the very company, Torzial, which will be in charge of the planning, development, and execution of the entire Larussio empire in Vegas after Carlos sells to Vicenti."

"Fuckin A... How did you get all that?" I ask.

"I can't tell you right now, maybe never, but rest assured the Chicago mafia knows that Jenny was laundering money for Mancini. They don't fucking care if she knew what she was doing or was being used by that piece of garbage or not. They just know that she may have information that could incriminate them and they want her out of the picture," he says.

"Fuck!"

"Exactly, they want to get rid of her because they think she can provide evidence of their guilt."

"How do we get her out of this?" I ask.

"We know Carlos wants to go legit and agreed to sell his family's share of the business to Vicenti, the biggest crime lord in South America. He intends to use this money to invest in a major block in Las Vegas and change his family's legacy. Mancini's been controlling the unions in that state and others for some time. The state approval for the Larussio builds should have been blocked by him as a favor for the Chicago mafia, but he hasn't had his eye on the ball and somehow Carlos was able to sneak by and already has approvals sealed up.

"That's all good, but you still haven't fucking told me how we get Jenny out of this situation," I say.

"It's complicated, hear me out," Matt says, taking a swig of his Coke.

My fucking patience is near the end but I nod. "Go ahead," I say.

"The Italian family knows her connection to Carlos and there's nothing short of a good old fashioned mafia war brewing. You probably know that Carlos Larussio wants out and has made a deal to sell to Vicenti, and in fact already has a plan to invest in Vegas. What you may not know is that Chase bought the adjoining properties in Vegas making the two families the largest stockholders on the strip," he says.

I don't tell him I already knew that from the report provided to me by Scottie, because I don't yet know how he fits into this or who to trust. "Interesting," I say.

"The Italian family is pissed and you've seen the way they retaliated against Carlos Larussio, their own flesh and blood."

"The good news is that they've just taken in Mancini, which means the Chicago mafia will be a bit more inclined to listen to and help us. What we need to focus on right now is an orchestrated plan to get the Chicago mafia on our side, and a defense for Jenny that doesn't bring criminal questions to their door. Until we do they're going to come after anyone and everyone to make this go away," he says, giving me a chin nod towards the door.

I know without a look around that Jenny is coming back in the room because my dick tightens every fucking time she gets close to me.

"We've already got Larry secured," Jay says, answering my next question before I ask.

"Good, keep him that way until after court," I say, looking at Jenny.

"It's been handled, Brian. We've scooped up his family for safekeeping as well," Jay says.

"Good work," I say, respecting the man for his foresight. I don't know how the fuck she makes yoga pants and one of her hoodie things look so hot, but she does and her freshly towel- dried hair makes me think of her in the shower with soap running down her body. I can feel my dick twitch and try to distract myself with pouring her a glass of wine.

"Thank you, Brian," she says and settles into the black leather sofa by the window overlooking the property.

"So please don't stop on my account. I need to hear this straight up. Tell me what I'm up against," she says.

I give Matt a chin nod and she narrows her eyes at me. She

likes that I'm in control in the bedroom, but still struggles with it outside of it. I have my work cut out for me.

"The last thing the Chicago mafia or Mancini want is for you to walk into that court- room. They don't know what you do or don't know at this point," Matt says.

"How does your security team fit into this Brian? If you guys hadn't come for me I wouldn't have had a chance," she says, shifting from side to side.

"Brian, I haven't had a chance to tell you this yet," Matt says, glancing up at me and around the room.

Matt, Jay, Paulie, and Jenny. I fucking trust them all and whatever he has to say we all need to know. "Guess now's as good a time as any," I say, bracing myself for exactly what I will hear about the man that has been like a second father to me since my father died.

"Jay's intel picked up several calls from Scottie's phone to the Larussio family in Italy. He was using a pretty sophisticated scrambling system, but Jay's team uncovered it. I know this must be hard to hear Brian and I'm sorry to be the one to tell you this, but if you have any doubt Jay's got tapes that he'll share with you," he says.

"Thanks, Matt. I realized the day of Jenny's hearing that something was off and that's the only fucking reason that I let Jenny go back to her condo. She was right that was the last place they would look for her. I'm the one that asked Jay's team to start an investigation on Scottie, but thinking that the man that treated you like a son may be guilty and hearing the worst confirmed are two different things," I say.

"I didn't realize the request came from you. It would definitely explain why he's been pushing the email correspondence between Mancini and Jenny that the police haven't brought forward, because it doesn't exist, and also explains the access to her computer during the time she was with you," Matt says.

"I know everyone's doing their best to help me, but with the Chicago mafia and Mancini after me and now Scottie and the Italian Larussio family involved, I don't think after the hearing that there's any doubt that they have enough evidence to make a case to send me to prison. In fact, I'm counting on it. I don't know what else to do except prepare for the worst," Jenny says, finishing the last sip of her wine to pour another.

Chapter 29

Jenny

HE THINKS HIS THREE DRINK RULE STILL APPLIES AFTER THE day I've had. I think not, and I finish pouring my second glass. "If you'll excuse me gentlemen, I was working on a project when I got the message about the security men being at my apartment. I really appreciate everything you did today to keep me safe. I need to finish a few things before it gets too late," I say, walking out of the room with the bottle of wine and a full glass in my hand. I don't need to look at him to feel the heat of his penetrating gaze following me until I reach the elevator. I hit the fifth floor button on the key pad.

I don't know why I feel a sense of calm in the total madness swirling around me, but it's clear to me that one of two things will happen. I will be sentenced to prison or I will be killed. There's no way the mafia is going to allow the person who laundered the money for the enforcer that embezzled it from them to walk free or talk about what she knows in court.

I pull up the document that I was working on when all hell

broke loose and begin reading through what's been written. Torzial Consulting will go to Katarina and Chase Prestian in the event of my death with monthly payments to my mother for the rest of her natural life. The money I have in savings will go to provide her with a brand new home, a new mini-van and be more than enough to take care of my nieces' and nephew's college. I was going to wait until my mom's birthday to let her pick out the house and van, but the reality that she may need to do this on her own weighs heavy on my heart as I take another sip of my wine. When I finish with the modifications to my will I save it and send it to Kate.

Message: Sending you a copy of my updated will. Please keep it safe.

Reply: Updating for any particular reason??

Message: Just in case- need to make sure my family is taken care of.

Reply: Try not to worry. Chase and Brian are working on it round the clock.

Message: In case I'm incarcerated will you take over Torzial until I get out?

Her response is immediate and I smile at the message.

Reply: Of course, but not necessary. You'll kick ass in court!

Message: Thanks for the vote of confidence!

My dearest friend Kate, always the optimist. After I have sent both documents to Kate I feel a momentary sense of relief and pour myself another drink. Now, I can work on the plan.

I look up my counselor's email and send her a note letting her know that the early morning flight to California will be unnecessary and that instead I am happy to talk to her on the telephone sometime tomorrow afternoon, instructing her to contact Brian for a secure phone number.

I take the last sip of my wine and hear the door softly open behind me. I don't need to turn around to know who it is because I can feel him, smell him, and my panties get wet just hearing him close the door and sensing him walking up behind me.

"How many glasses of wine have you had?" he asks, caressing the sensitive skin of my nape with his fingers.

"Only three," I say.

"But when you took the bottle and flashed your disobedient little eyes at me you were intending to drink more?"

"I'm not going to lie to you. I'm still planning to take another drink," I say.

"Very well, we've at least progressed from outright sneaking around to being able to voice your needs. You've been a very naughty girl Sweetheart and as a result have had a very traumatic day," he says, sliding his tongue into the crevice of my ear causing goosebumps to rise on my arms and my pussy to clench.

"I won't allow you to have another drink and then be punished, but if you choose to play I'll give you another drink afterwards," he says.

I shiver with the anticipation and moan softly. "I need to hear the words, Sweetheart. Do you want to be punished for being such a bad girl and putting yourself in danger?" he asks.

"Yes, I want you to punish me Brian," I say.

He spins me around. "I like that you didn't hesitate and that you're learning to express your desires. Come with me," he says, taking my hand and leading me down the hall to the elevator. The door closes and he chooses LL on the keypad, watching me intently as we descend.

"Tonight you can explore and ask me anything you want," he says as we exit into the lower level. I take in the large room we walk through, which has multiple tables and chairs throughout the space, love seats scattered throughout, and four, six foot birdcage-like structures hanging from the ceiling. The bar along the expanse of the far wall is similar to the one upstairs, but instead of one large monitor it has eight monitors displayed overhead.

"Questions?" he asks, taking my hand in his.

"Umm, not yet," I say, trying to keep up to him.

He keeps hold of my hand as he guides me down the very long hall, past many closed doors, but open windows allow me to see the variety of rooms and equipment within each. My heart is pounding with unleashed excitement and I hope the sound of our steps against the stone floor drown out the heaviness of my breathing.

"Take it all in," he says, pausing to open the door at the end of the hall. My heart beats so loudly I think he may be able to hear it thumping inside of my chest when I see the St. Andrew's cross, floggers, whips and canes displayed in the room.

"I take it you like that," he says, caressing my nape as he guides me down the hall to the next room equipped with a black spanking bench that has restraint devices for wrists and ankles. It's not like I haven't seen this on websites, but none as plush and luxurious as this one adorned in leather and a head cushion and absolutely none that I've been in the same room with. The thought of being sprawled out on this device with my hands and legs bound and getting spanked by Brian is exciting to me.

"I can see the desire in your eyes, your heart rate has changed and I can smell your pussy from here," he says.

"I can't deny anything that you say," I say.

"Let's continue to explore then," he says.

I nod, as he walks me toward another room. "Tell me what you think of this, Sweetheart," he says, guiding me into it.

The bed in the middle of the room has wrought iron head and footboards with multiple elegant curls and hooks and no covers, just a plain purple mattress. There are implements hanging on the walls around the room, floggers, bull whips, canes, paddles, and the table next to the bed displays an assortment of dildos and butt plugs. I shiver, unable to control my body's desire and anticipation of what's to come.

"I hear the change in your breathing. Tell me what you like," he says, guiding me into the room.

"Everything, it's everything I could imagine and then some," I say.

"Are you ready to experiment and to accept your punishment?" he asks, caressing my cheek and kissing me, parting my lips with his tongue.

I moan. "I want to know what you're thinking. Do the things you see turn you on?" he says, capturing my eyes with that blue crystalline gaze.

"Yes, I like this room very much," I breathe as he closes the door behind me.

"Normally these rooms are visible from the hall and the monitors at the bar, but I have no intention of allowing anyone to see you undressed but me," he says, hitting a button on the side of the door that brings the shades down over the windows to the hall.

"Strip for me and take your time. I want to enjoy this," he says, guiding me further into the room.

I begin slowly and inch by inch pull my hoodie up, gently caressing the path that my hands have just left exposed. I reach my breasts and expose the white see through lace bra and when I see his look of satisfaction it only spurs me on. I slow down, knowing it's turning him on before lifting the top completely from my frame and over my head.

"You are a little seductress aren't you? You've done that well, now let the lace that covers those delectable little tits fall to the ground. Show me now," he says.

My sex clenches with desire at his command and I unclip the

snap in the front and slowly pull the material apart to expose my nipples to his view.

"So fucking perfect," he says, caressing first one and then both nipples with his fingers. He pushes another button on the wall causing soft and sultry sounds to emanate throughout the room. "I want to finish undressing you, expose your pussy," he says, sliding his hands into the waistband of my yoga pants. "So beautiful Sweetheart, and you didn't wear panties. Open your legs for me, Jenny," he says, pushing me gently onto the soft rubbery mattress.

"Any issues with restraints tonight?" he says, brushing his lips against mine.

I shake my head. "No, I want this. I need this," I say as he kisses me on the lips and then dips lower.

"Slide up, I want to bind you to my bed," he says, affixing the soft cuffs around my wrists and then to the ornate hooks in the headboard.

The intensity of his stare heats my skin and I do as he instructs, delighting in the flash of desire that passes over his otherwise stoic face as my legs fall apart exposing the most intimate part of my body.

"Good girl, now stay still for me," he says, restraining both of my ankles through the soft anklets and then to the circles in the footboard.

"What's your safe word?" he asks and I know that he believes I will be challenged tonight. I breathe deeply; I have an overwhelming desire to experience where he wants to take me at least one time.

"Red, but I won't use it," I say.

"I should take away your sight so that you can experience the deep anxiety I felt when you walked out and you didn't answer my calls, but I think it may be too much too soon little one. Tonight you need to be able to see me," he says, brushing my lips with a kiss.

He is fully dressed in his suit pants, but removes his black suit jacket throwing it casually over the chair next to us before loosening his tie and top button of his shirt. He begins a search of the room, selecting a flogger, leather belt, a long bull whip and then reaches for the cane from the corner of the room.

My heart begins beating rapidly, my mouth is dry and as he walks toward me with them he watches me intently. I turn to avert my eyes, hoping he won't see the pure unadulterated fear that I know must be visible.

"Look at me, at all times, unless I instruct you differently. I want to see your fear, that is an honest reaction for someone who has never experienced anything of this nature," he says, laying his instruments of choice on the small rectangular table beside the bottom of the bed.

"In a relationship such as ours trust is critical. Tell me how these implements make you feel," he says, taking the flogger from the table and allowing the strands to gently glide over my feet, all the way up my legs, allowing the strands to drape my sex before moving across my stomach and nipples. "Tell me," he says, allowing them to tease my erect nipples.

"Scared, but turned on and curious," I say, hoarsely.

"As it should be little one," he says, laying the flogger back on the table and picking up a long black leather belt. He doubles it in two sections and cracks it between his hands and the sound resonates through the room.

"I need to hear you, Jenny. We're getting to the point of no return. How does this belt make you feel?" he says, cracking it again.

I start... and in that moment I know this is not what I want. I may have thought being tied down and spanked with a belt or caned is what I wanted, but... "I don't like the look of it or the thought of it hitting my body," I murmur softly, trying desperately to avoid those deep penetrating blue eyes.

"I see," he says and if this is what he likes I know in this moment that I'll never be the one to satisfy him.

"And how does this one make you feel? Hot, wet, bothered?" he asks, running the tip of the cane across my nipples, lightly tapping them with it before descending over my navel and tapping on my mound. The erotic feel of it over my nipples is undeniable, but I can't silence the fear in my head of being hit with it and the tears begin slowly until I can no longer contain them.

"Tell me all the emotions that ran through your mind," he says, placing the cane on the table with the other implements, leaning next to me and wiping the tears from my face.

I look into his eyes, they are icy blue and more than I fear the instruments, the feeling of loss to come is overwhelming to me. "I felt exposed, anxious, nervous, then outright scared— well maybe petrified once the cane came out," I say, trying to avert my eyes, but he tilts my chin to prevent it and places the toy in his hand next to my sex turning it on low.

"The vibrations are different when you're all tied up and can't move away from their pulses."

I can't help but cry out at the overwhelming sensations, but in this position am unable to move away from it.

"Those are some of the same emotions that I felt when you disappeared, but you left out helpless, powerless, vulnerable, and weak," he says, turning the vibrator on full speed.

I cry out, writhing and caught up with the sensation of the build, but he pulls it away and my impending climax disappears and I sigh in frustration. "I'm sorry, Brian. I didn't intend for you to feel that way."

"What are you more scared of than those instruments? I want you to tell me," he says, starting the heavenly little pulsing again.

My hips rise up of their own accord. No sense beating around the bush or putting the inevitable off. "Losing you," I say softly.

"You think you will lose me why?" he asks.

I shake my head unable to respond with the sensations of the climax so near, but once again he removes it and I cry out in despair. "Because the instruments that you showed me scare me," I say, trying my best to blink the tears away but unable to. They fall down my cheeks unrestricted and I feel my entire body and soul constrict with the hurt.

"You see one thing like an arm casually placed around a person for a picture and assume I'm fucking someone I told you I didn't have feelings for and then just a mere day later you see me show you a few instruments and decide I'm a sadist and we're no longer compatible? You think that's a healthy trusting relationship?"

"No, but ..." I say and his icy blue eyes flash and narrow at me.

"But what? Don't think, Jenny. I want to know what makes you react like that. Don't think, just let your feelings flow. Tell me now," he urges.

"Why me? You can have any girl you want. Sasha is beautiful, poised and you said you broke your rules for her," I say, trying desperately not to let him see my tears.

"I think until about thirty seconds ago I thought I might give you another word to consider, but I see that I was wrong. Your issue is not trust so much as self-worth in this respect and I'm going to enjoy making you realize just how fucking worthy you are," he says, kissing my tears before traveling the length of my body with his lips, past my ear lobe, across my collar- bone and paying special attention to my nipples which are still erect and needy. He warms one in his mouth before he nibbles with his teeth and it goes straight to my sex. His blue eyes flash with awareness and he travels lower, dipping his warm tongue in my navel causing me to squirm with need.

"Still or I'll tie your waist down," he growls, heading lower and rubbing my mound with his fingers, tapping lightly on it, heightening my awareness of it before lowering his mouth and touching my clit with his tongue. The slightest caress, but my body is strung out and I raise my hips in need.

"What did I say about moving? If you do it again, I'll be done, and I'll bind your hands so you can't touch yourself tonight," he says, looking up at me with wicked glass blue eyes.

"Brian, I can't take it," I moan.

"That's it Sweetheart, just stay still and let the feeling center you, all you have to do is feel me and forget about everything else," he says, grasping my ass and pulling me into his mouth as he takes hold of my clit, suckling until I am bucking in his arms. "Come for me right now," he demands and the waves that have been building come crashing down around me. "Brian, please stop," I plead, crying out his name as wave after wave crashes around me.

I vaguely feel my legs lifted over his shoulders. I didn't even hear his zipper come down but I can feel him hard, rigid and needy at the edge of my entrance. "Ready Sweetheart?" he asks.

I nod but that's not good enough. "I need to hear you," he says, wrapping himself and rubbing along the slippery wetness and making me edge closer to him.

"Ready," I say, gasping, unprepared for the depth the position brings and the way he hits that special little spot deep inside of me, over and over, both absorbed in the impending connection of our orgasm until he pushes us over the edge and we slowly begin to come back to earth.

He uncuffs my hands and pulls me against him. "Now, I think

you deserve the indulgence in another glass of wine, but don't think you'll get that often. The three drink rule will apply after tonight," he says.

Chapter 30

Brian

I LOOK DOWN AT HER SLEEPING FRAME AND I WANT NOTHING more than to climb in next to her and feel her body next to mine, but not here. I slip on my pants and lift her in the blanket she's wrapped in and head for the elevator. She nuzzles into my chest and I smile as even in her subconscious she finds my beating heart like she's drawn to it no matter what.

As soon as I lay her in my bed and pull the covers over her my phone buzzes alerting me that they've got Larry on the line. I text that I'll be there momentarily and head into the bathroom feeling a sense of loss as I wash her scent from my skin and rinse her taste out of my mouth. I give her sleeping body one last glance before I head downstairs. We're down to two weeks to figure out how to navigate this trial and I need my fucking head in the game.

Jay and Matt have created a mini conference room and have blueprints of something laid out all over the bar and the secure phone is lit up and lying on top. Jay hits the button to unmute the call when I walk in. "Larry, Brian's here," he says.

"Brian, they've got me holed up in some goddamned cabin and won't let me see my family. What gives?" he says.

"Larry, they're protecting you. Ever since you walked into my condo with that damned envelope things have heated up. I tried to make sure they thought it contained information that incriminated Jenny and not them or the mafia, but they went after her anyways. They're not taking any chances and Matt got you and your family to safety about ten minutes before they crashed in the door to your home," I say.

"Dammit! Where are they? I have to know they're safe," he says.

"Larry, you have my word they are, and the security teams will continue to make sure of that, but after this is over you're going to need new identities," I say.

"I started liquidating assets awhile back in the event something like this happened," he says.

"Larry, you're defending the woman I love. I have more money than I could piss away in a hundred years without even touching the interest-bearing accounts that my grandfather left my father. You and your family will never have to worry about money for as long as you live. I promise you that," I say.

"Alright, show me proof that my wife and family are safe and then let's get down to business. Can you set up a secure Skype or is that too techy for your goons?" he says.

I have a hard time controlling my smirk as Matt's face turns red at the insult and Jay shakes his head at the young security agent as he begins typing into the secure system to set up a connection. I hit the mute button all of a sudden cold with the realization that someone else is with Larry. Matt couldn't have left him alone if he has access to a computer. They wouldn't be able to control who he contacts.

"Matt while you're figuring that out I need a word with Jay

about Chase and the Larussios. Excuse us for a moment," I say, gesturing to Jay to follow me outside onto the patio overlooking the expanse of garden.

"He's not alone if he's got access to a computer. Who the fuck is with Larry?" I say, as soon as we're outside.

"Keith, he's loyal and nothing would make him break Chase's trust. Chase brought him home from overseas assignments when his wife was getting close to delivering their child, and bought them a home when the little arrived."

I know that Chase is kind hearted and his employees would do anything for him, but I also know that Scottie was the same. My father treated him like a brother and I treated him like an uncle and then a father after my own died. There's nothing monetarily that he didn't have. "Anyone can be bought. Why didn't Matt tell me that Larry wasn't alone?" I say.

"I told him not to tell you anything about the arrangement. If you were captured, for Jenny's sake, it was better that you knew nothing. They have ways of making grown men talk against their will," he says.

If I didn't know it before in an instant I know that if something happens to me, Jenny will be protected to the best of his ability. I extend my hand and he has the good grace to acknowledge it. "I've been a fucking ass to you and your men and I apologize. I was worried about Jenny, but that's no excuse for the way I've treated you. It's clear from what you've just told me that you won't compromise her safety in any way, shape, or form and I'm deeply grateful," I say.

Jay looks uncomfortable, but shakes my hand. "Jay, have you ever been in a committed relationship? No need to answer, but can you let Larry talk to his wife, even for a short time without putting Jenny at risk?" I ask.

He nods. "Let me see what I can do," he says.

"Oh, and Jay," I say.

"Yeah Brian?"

"Thanks for everything you've done for the people that I care about. I know why Chase holds you in such high regard," I say.

"You're welcome, anytime," he says as we walk back into the living room where Matt and Larry are talking to each other.

"Are you sure it's secure?" I say.

"It is now, we've scrambled the transmissions a few times to the point it will be impossible to follow or trace it, but we won't push our luck. Let's keep it at minute intervals, scramble and then reconvene," Matt says.

"Got it," I say, sitting on the bar stool watching Larry on the overhead monitor.

"Larry, I know it's not the best of situations, but are you comfortable?" I ask.

"I'm fine, just worried about my family," Larry says.

"I can only imagine," I say, wondering if I would ever even survive if I thought Jenny was in danger and wasn't in a position to help her.

"Your family is safe and we'll get you in contact with them as soon as we're done with this call. I can never repay you enough for tipping me off to the fact that Scottie was dirty and the mafia had sights set on Jenny. In the meantime, let's talk about next steps," I say.

"I'm not going to sugar coat this. It will be hard to make the jury believe Jenny didn't know anything about the millions of dollars being laundered through her own company. The fact she's best friends with the daughter of the largest crime lord on the east coast doesn't help her situation. I'm counting on them trying to make a case that Ty's demise was a purchased service by her. If they go that way we have a counter," Larry says.

"You know most of Carlos Larussio's businesses are legit,"

Jenny says, walking into the room. I glance at the clock, it's late, early morning really and she's barely had an hour of sleep.

"Unfortunately that hasn't always been the case and what the city and the potential jurors know about him is that he is mafia and you are best friends with his daughter," Larry says.

"I've been best friends with his daughter for years, she hasn't known him long and I just met him at the wedding," she says.

"Exactly, it's also the same night we met and I knew how shocked you were when I told you who I was. That wasn't faked and I damn well know it so when Scottie said you knew who I was long before that time it was just one more reason to question his loyalty and motives," I say.

She nods. "I met you both that night," she says.

"I know, but the prosecutor will spin this if he's doing his job. The fact that Torzial was laundering money is irrefutable. The fact that you left Ty's with a split lip the night he was discovered taking money from the pharm and unions, didn't come back to his condo after that, and started counseling after that are all things that just build the prosecutor's story. Then add in your journal where in just about every nightly entry there is a reference to wanting him dead. I'm going to be honest with everyone here. We're gonna have to play hard ball and shit's about to get real," Larry says.

"Tell me something I wanna hear, Larry," I say, watching Jenny's face visibly pale.

"Here's the plan. I'm going to let them believe there's a chance you may change your mind and plea bargain, even though that time should have been over. I want them to think this case is a slam dunk."

"I'm not pleading guilty to something that I didn't do," Jenny says, her eyes flashing.

"No, you won't, but we need to give them a sense of confidence that what they've laid out is good enough for us to want to plea bargain instead of going to court with them. I'm hoping this keeps them from digging any further or concocting any other ways of trying to make you look guilty or worse," Larry says and I swallow hard knowing they'll come for her if we don't get this right.

"Okay, that makes sense," she says, but she's looking a little lost.

"Then we're going to make friends with the mafia," he says.

"You're gonna do fucking what?" I say, pushing my chair back and standing up to look into the monitor and wishing he were in the room so I could throttle him.

"We're going to turn the tables. They're going to make your affiliation with the mafia a

credibility issue and a means of having a hit put out on Ty," Larry says.

"Yeah, they're going to do exactly that and we're going to let them," I say.

"Hear me out, Brian. I am systematically going to review every piece of Mancini's

deposits to Ty. They are irrefutable pieces of evidence. Jay and his team made sure of it the night things went down. The court can't deny that everything done was initiated by Ty even though Jenny's signatures were on some of the documents. We are then going to protect the Chicago mafia by showcasing Mancini for what he was. We will uncover that he was embezzling money from the unions and hard working men and women that paid their dues in the city of Chicago. We will then paint the story that Mancini was running it through Ty and his girlfriend's company unbeknownst to her and we will show that the last entry was shortly before that fateful night," Larry says.

She's shaking her head. "No, what about all the entries in the Torzial accounting books since then," she says.

"Jenny, Brian has been having the teams trying to find one shred of evidence that could be used against you. It doesn't exist. The deposits to the accounts stopped ..." he says, and I cut him off.

"Sweetheart, the day Scottie came to court and tried to convince me that you weren't the person I knew, the doubts I've been having about him were confirmed. I know you Sweetheart, I know your heart and as soon as I got past the initial shock I knew he was guilty, but I wasn't sure what his motivation was and I didn't want him to have a reason to come after you," I say.

"You let me believe you thought I was guilty," she says and she looks away. It's not a submissive look, but dismissive in nature.

I need to connect with her, for her to look at me, but she's avoiding eye contact at all costs. "I needed time to process and to get a plan together," I say, lifting her chin and kissing her lightly on the lips.

Larry coughs. "If you two are both done, maybe we could focus on the plan. We'll show the first attack that left Ty almost dead with the Larussio markings was at the hands of Tony Larussio and then we'll make the connection between him and the Italian family and their hate for the New York Larussio family. We will then show the connection between the Italian family and Mancini and show that he had the most to gain by removing the person that could prove he was embezzling money from the unions," Larry says.

I've been trying to control my temper but I can't any longer. "You're putting her right in the fucking middle of a fucking mafia war," I explode.

"There's no other way around this," Larry says.

"Fuck!"

"I know this isn't sitting well with you Brian and what I'm

about to say next is likely to infuriate you too, but it's my job to figure this shit out."

I nod, giving him the silent go ahead knowing he needs answers if he's going to put a plausible defense together.

"Jenny, I don't have an angle yet to explain the email between yourself and Mancini asking you to meet with him to discuss union options for the Prestian Corp medical facilities and Las Vegas holdings. You and Brian have both told me it doesn't exist, but I need to know what I'm going to see in that letter if they produce it as evidence and what happened in the meeting that you supposedly set up with Mancini if you did," Larry says.

"I can't help you because it doesn't exist. Brian asked me the same thing and I do recall getting a voicemail by someone with that last name, but I didn't have a chance to listen to it. I was asleep and missed the call. I didn't recognize it and dialed it back the next morning. All I got was a recording that kept transferring me from one recording to another. I was barely awake and hung up. I sort of forgot all about it until he asked me about it. If they produce a letter it's fabricated."

"This was on your cell phone?"

"Yep, it's the only phone I use," she responds.

"Jenny, if his name showed up on your phone then he was in your contact list," Larry says and I watch as she digests this.

Instead of replying she pulls her phone out and swipes through her lists of contacts. She scrolls and scrolls before she finally stops and I watch the color drain right the fuck out of her face.

"It's still there," she says barely above a whisper, shaking her head. "You have to believe me, I didn't put his contact name in my telephone, I didn't get an email from him, and I most certainly did not reply to one or set up a meeting with him to talk about the private affairs of Carlos Larussio," she says.

Matt pushes his chair back from the table and begins pacing. "Let's take a step back. The day you were attacked Ty told you that he was loading stuff on your computer.

She is resolute and her eyes flash. "I don't know how else to explain it," she says and I see the deflated look in her eyes and want to punch something.

"Jay, who on your team did you have working on this?" I ask.

"Matt was gone, Scottie's team said he'd handle it while we were working on everything else," Jay says, pausing as what he's just said registers with everyone around the table.

"Fuck!"

"Matt, let's get Chase's people on it and see if we can trace the hack."

"Roger that," Matt says, immediately starting to type into his cell.

"Larry do you think they're going to let you have the journal thrown out?" I ask.

"I'm working with the counselor and trying to find precedence for it. In this particular case though we're getting hung up on the fact that it specifically states method of demise and matches the murder identically," he says.

"You mean the comment about wishing he were castrated?" I ask.

"Let's be completely clear here," he says, pushing his lenses onto the top of his head. "I mean the multiple references to not only wishing he were dead, but that his dick was cut off and shoved in his own mouth," he says and Jenny turns even whiter.

"I did write that and I meant every word of it, but I didn't do it or hire anyone to," she says and I watch her deep green eyes as she processes this.

"Larry, we're done for the night. Keep me apprised and in the meantime let me know if there's anything that you think I can do to be of assistance," I say.

"The only thing I need right now is to talk to my family and make sure with my own eyes and ears that they're okay," he says.

"Jay and Matt will have you connected with them within the hour, Larry. Thanks for all you're doing. You have my word we will keep them safe," I say, before disconnecting and watching Jenny walk over to the wine bottle.

She looks up at me and I nod and she pours herself a drink and thanks the team for their efforts. The day couldn't have been worse for her emotionally and I can feel the anxiety pouring off of her even as she acts like she's holding it together. She's going to need to learn to let me take care of things for her in the future and that's exactly what I intend to teach her tonight.

"Matt, Jay," thank you for everything today. Celia has flown in for the duration and is one floor above in the kitchen. She'll have rooms prepared for your overnight stay," I say, taking the bottle and another glass from the bar, and leading her to the elevator.

I pull her close to me, putting my arms around her, not knowing how she has managed to creep into my body and soul. I watch her trying to pretend that everything is okay and when she sees me hit the lower level button I see the spark in her eye. That's right, Sweetheart we're going to play a bit.

We pass by the room with the spanking horse and I can't help notice the lovely little blush crawling up the sides of her cheeks and my dick twitches at the image of her nude and spread for me. "When we explore that room I'll see if I can warm your ass cheeks to the same pretty little color of your blush, but tonight I have other plans," I say as I guide her past it. Her eyes flash in a tell of disappointment and I make note not to make her wait too long.

I guide her down the hall and open one of the doors on the left. The room has two massage tables on one side, and a gentle glow is flickering from the candles that are lit around the kidney shaped pool and a heavenly scent of lavender wafts through the entire room.

"It's a mineral oil bath. Take a sip of your wine. I want to taste its sweetness from your mouth," I say, tilting the drink to her lips before capturing them and exploring her depths with my tongue. I feel the heat of her pushing into me and all I want to do is take her away from the pain of the day.

"Undress for me," I say, setting her wine on the table next to us. She looks into my eyes and my cock twitches before she even begins to remove her sweater. She's taking it slow, teasing me, allowing me to enjoy little glimpses of her belly and the dainty lace that barely covers the swell of her breasts, but I won't allow her to focus on pleasing me when my goal is to take her away from all of the worries that have been plaguing her.

She pauses, her deep green eyes uncertain. I see the emotions of the day swirling and can see that she's not sure how to react. Her shoulders slump and I watch her eyes drop to the floor.

Fuck me. My cock twitches and expands with need. "When I ask you to undress do it quickly, now turn around so I can see your beautiful body," I say, relishing in the way her breath hitches. The woman that is normally so cool and composed is at a dead end tonight and I am going to make sure she doesn't have one minute to focus on her fears.

I unclip the little hook and remove the dainty straps from her shoulders, enjoying her shivering at my control. She's sexy as hell and normally I would relax and enjoy the show, but tonight is about her. "Pull it over your head and turn around," I say, rubbing my fingers over her erect pink nipples before lowering to her waistband and sliding her pants and panties down. "Slip into the pool and let me watch you," I say.

Chapter 31

Jenny

I LET MY BODY SUBMERGE TO MY SHOULDERS IN THE SOFT, warm silky water while in one flick of the switch he dims the overhead lights and the candle-like lights surrounding the pool become iridescent. He undresses slowly, tossing his suit coat on the table, and unfastens his tie. "We can make good use of this later," he says, throwing it next to his jacket, loosening his cuff links, and placing them on the table before unbuttoning his shirt to join it.

My breath hitches. His chest is muscular and lean but not bulky, and when he unfastens his dress pants and lets them and his Jockeys fall to the ground my sex quivers. His nakedness is riveting and I watch him walk toward the pool. His thighs flex and the power behind those muscles and his erect cock make my sex wet with need. He is watching me with an intensity that sets my body on fire, causing everything south to clench before he slips into the pool.

"You're so tense, Sweetheart," he says, capturing the sensitive skin of my ear lobe.

I moan, leaning into him. "I'm going to teach you to breathe. I can feel the anxiety rolling off of you in waves. First you need to get into Tai Chi posture," he says, standing upright.

I start to ask him what it is, but he shakes his head. "Spread your feet, shoulder width apart. Follow my lead," he instructs, kissing my lips.

"Bend your knees and keep them soft. There you go, now let your tailbone drop. That's it Sweetheart, relax your chest and shoulders, and pretend that beautiful creamy neck is slowly being pulled upward, and you should be able to feel the stretch all over."

I nod, feeling the release in my neck and my entire body.

"Breathe in deeply allowing the oxygen to fill and expand your belly, now release. This enables the release of carbon dioxide out of your body." I do as he asks and watch as our breathing syncs. "Now add movement," he says, raising his arms overhead.

"Inhale as we go up, and exhale as we come down," he says.

"Good girl, again," he says until both our breathing and movements are in sync. I don't know how long it's been when I hear his voice again, but I feel completely at peace and relaxed.

"Come with me," he says, caressing my cheek, helping me out of the pool, and toweling me off gently before guiding me to the massage table.

"Your body is still tense, lay face down," he says, covering me with a lightweight but freshly warmed blanket as I do.

I push my face into the warmth of the massage table and try not to focus on anything that has gone on in the last few weeks.

"There, practice your breathing, deep inhale and then exhale, careful not to force your exhales, let it flow naturally," he says, gently instructing me.

At his guidance, I don't hesitate placing my head into the cushiony face space as he pushes the hair away from my neck and rubs my nape.

"Mmm... so good," I moan.

"Focus on my hands, Sweetheart," he says, kneading my neck with his thumbs as a light lilting voice begins to play overhead and the lights dim further and he slowly removes the blanket, leaving me completely nude.

"So beautiful, Sweetheart, now you're going to feel a different type of warmth. The heat from the stones will penetrate your muscles and allow you to release tension and stress much better," he says, rubbing oil on my back.

"Brian, this is so good," I say.

"The consistency is different than some essential oils you may have experienced in massage, it's unscented grapeseed oil," he says before working the heat of the rocks over my body, allowing the heat to penetrate, but removing them before they become too hot.

I don't tell him that I've never had a massage, that the thought of a stranger touching me so intimately has never appealed, but once the rhythm starts I hear myself softly moan. I snuggle my face deeper in the cushions, allowing my arms to rest in the luxurious side cushions as he works his magic on my neck, shoulders, and back for what must be over an hour.

I am barely aware of the electric table repositioning my body until he begins kissing the sensitive underside of my neck, slowly licking upward toward the sensitive skin of my earlobe.

"Close your eyes and just feel my hands," he says, stroking me, letting his hands explore my body, down the sensitive curve of my neck and spine and then over the curves of my ass before gently flipping me onto my back. "Tell me what you feel when I stroke your body like this," he says, rubbing my nipples with his fingers, gently rolling them between his thumbs.

"I like it," I moan as it sends a need deep inside of my center.

"I know you like it Sweetheart; tell me what it is that you feel. Tell me how your little pussy feels when I stroke you or how it feels when I do this," he says, using his tongue to blaze a trail of heat from my erect and aching nipples, down to my belly.

"Mmm, so good, Brian," I say, rising up.

"I need to taste how sweet you are," he says before allowing his tongue to wash over me with the slowest of touches, my body heats and he continues stroking me with his tongue and I can't control the desire or my body's response as it begins trembling with pent up desire and need for release. "Good girl, spread your legs and let me have what's mine. That delectable creamy center is what I want, Sweetheart. Do it now," he instructs, his tongue dipping into my trembling center. My thighs quiver with overstimulation trying to close on their own account, but he holds them apart watching me as his tongue dips inside of me and then slowly drags over my clit, slowly but repeatedly.

When he sucks hard I moan aloud, unable to control the building waves. He continues to suck and the sensation is too much and pulls me trembling around him. "Stop, no more, I can't come anymore," I moan.

He kisses my mound gently, sliding me to the bottom of the table. I watch as he rubs his unprotected cock on my mound. "I want no barriers between us from now on, emotional or physical. You're protected and we've both been cleared. I want to feel you, skin on skin," he says and I moan my consent right before he enters me. He lifts my legs over the top of his shoulders, grasping my waist to bring me closer, driving himself deep and slow. I moan at the depth the position allows and gasp as he hits that special place deep inside of me. He smiles at me as my hips rise of their own accord and he starts to rebuild my desire.

"One more time, Sweetheart," he says, as I shake my head unable to control the impending waves.

"It's so good," I say, panting, and when he begins driving

deeper, I'm right there, can feel it building and with a deep thrust I shatter around him and he pulls out rubbing his shaft a couple more times as he releases on the top of my skin, my mound, and all over my belly.

Chapter 32

Brian

I LOOK DOWN AT THE COME I'VE SHOT ALL OVER HER BODY and give my dick one last squeeze making sure that every last bit is on her skin. Commitment has never been my thing, but for some unknown reason I not only want this woman as mine I want to mark her as such, and even that is not enough, I want my scent on her skin, my marks on her body. The thought of losing her is messing with my head. I rub my come into her delicate white skin. "Vitamin E is good for you," I say, smirking at the mess I've made.

She's looking at me with that doll-like appearance, and I know she's drifting. I clean her up and get another blanket out of the warming station and lay it across her, kissing her lips gently before sliding into my pants and lifting her into my arms. I take the back elevator that leads directly to my room and nod at the security man right outside.

I lay her body in my own bed, the first woman that has ever been in this room. I had the rooms designed to ensure that whatever me or my Cali friends desired could be accommodated and it seldom included having a sexual companion join you in your own room afterward. I make a mental note to take her to all of my homes across the world and break them in right.

I place her onto the bed, blanket and all, and then pull the comforter over the top of her knowing as her body comes down she'll chill. I strip my clothes off and pull her back into the warmth of my body. She fucking purrs and wiggles in next to me. I pull her close, nuzzling her neck, relishing in the feel of the long silky strands of hair against my skin. Her breathing becomes even and I know she's completely relaxed and in for a long deep sleep. I look down at her and realize how close I came to losing her because she thought I desired another and that now I may lose her to an even deeper injustice.

The phone buzzes next to my computer and I pick it up, taking a sip of the coffee that Celia has laid out on the breakfast table for me while I work.

"Jay here. We've got everything in place for the trial next week. She'll have the best security, but we need to integrate Scottie and his team. I personally don't think they've been buying the, 'I'm on vacation and want to be alone to get to the bottom of her betrayal' for a short while. I got word that a few of the newscasters are feeling the pressure to release the stories. If that newspaper article comes out today, they're going to know you're moving her and that she'll be back in Chicago for the hearing next week."

"I'll call Scottie. Let him know that I needed some time with her to get my head around the fact that she's guilty, get her out of my system if you will, and that I'm planning to haul her ass into court next week," I say, glancing up as I feel her and the look on her face makes me physically sick. Fuck, she's turning white as a ghost right before my eyes and she whips around before I can stop her, taking off in the direction of the elevator. It's almost closed shut before my foot stops it. The doors reopen and she moves away from me, to the back of the elevator, tears running uncontrolled down her face.

"Jenny, listen to me. I didn't mean a word of that," I say, running my hand through my hair. How the fuck am I supposed to explain this. "What you heard was me talking to Jay about what I plan to tell Scottie. We think he's dirty Jenny, but we need more time to figure out what he's up to," I say, closing the gap between us in two long strides.

"You told Jay and Matt that I was guilty," she says, pushing against my chest as I try to wrap her in my arms.

"I made my entire team think you were guilty to protect you, but it wasn't enough. They still came after you the other night, which confirms that Scottie's probably working for the mafia, but we need to be sure and keep you safe while Jay and Matt are getting it sorted. Scottie knows how much I care about you. Telling him I brought you here to get you out of my system was the only plausible thing I could think of."

"Is that what you were doing last night? Getting me out of your system?" she says in barely a whisper, and she's still avoiding my eyes.

"Look at me," I say and she slowly raises her face. The depth of uncertainty in those deep green eyes kills me. She has been hurt so badly. I cover her mouth with my own, pulling her into me. It takes everything I have not to restrain her arms and push them up the wall and pin my body against hers.

She moans against me and opens willingly and I walk her back slowly towards the wall. Why this woman should trust me, the most callous of men, someone that has used women for pleasure and nothing more all of his life, but at this particular moment that is all I want, her trust. "Lift your arms for me, Jenny," I say, coaxing her.

I can hear the sound of her breath shallow and my dick twitches every time she inhales deeply, steeling herself. "Arms up Sweetheart," I say, testing, half expecting her to kick me in the balls and hightail it out of the elevator. She's pensive and afraid, but she extends her arms, overcoming her fear and it's right there that I know somehow I need to find it in myself to do the same.

I guide her out of the elevator and scoop her into my arms, carrying her down the hallway to my bedroom. I lift her the night-gown over her head, and lay her onto the bed wanting to devour every inch of her nude body with my desire. The creamy silkiness of her skin, the dark chestnut hair falling around her little heart-shaped face is enticing and she's looking expectantly at me with those baby doll eyes.

"You're so brave Sweetheart," I murmur, kissing her on the lips. She tastes of lingering toothpaste and her hair smells like mangos, the scent that stays with me, on my clothes, long after she's done nuzzling into my chest or sleeping in my bed. I break away gently, undressing before sliding in next to her, pulling her to me and capturing her lips.

I taste the saltiness of her tears and break our kiss, wiping them from her eyes. "I'm not so brave, Brian," she says.

"Sshh. You're braver than anyone I know. You've gone through so much and you've shouldered it alone for too long."

"When I heard you say I was guilty and that you were getting me out of your system, I believed it. I believed the worst about you and Sasha and didn't give you a chance to explain. You don't deserve to have someone in your life that doesn't trust you completely," she says, wiping the tears that are pooling from her eyes.

"You've gone through one of the worst experiences a woman

can endure. The man you trusted to be a life partner abused and hurt you. Give yourself time, I will," I say, capturing her lips with my own.

I'm in my study hours later when my cell rings. "Brian here," I say, taking a pull from my coffee.

"It's Larry and I'm afraid it isn't with good news. We need to discuss the strategy around the journal. I've reworked it time and time again and I'm just not feeling confident," he says.

"Fuck!" I say loudly enough that Celia pops her head in from the kitchen and seeing nothing of alarm just as quickly disappears to whatever she was doing.

"Is she around? I need to speak with her, prepare her for the changes," he says.

"She's in the shower. Give me some time to think of a way to break this to her," I say, swallowing hard because I know her entire fucking life is riding on this.

"Tell me you've got a plan, one that will work, Larry," I say.

"I do, but it would have been better if they had disallowed it. We've known we may have to resort to this for a while so I've been narrowing down a panel of expert psychologists. We're going to need to bring one of them on board. The one with the most experience and best trial outcomes in cases like this is the most expensive one we've found. She's also halfway around the world right now and we're going to need to get her stateside as soon as possible to get her brought up to speed if she's going to have any chance of helping. We thought the judge would allow us to move the trial, but it looks like community pressure is on and they want this done fast."

"I don't give a damn about the expense. Do what you need to

do and let me know when you have it arranged," I say, disconnecting. It takes me all of five minutes to realize that I'm not willing to bet Jenny's freedom on little miss psychologist; I don't care how fucking good the world thinks she is. We're going to need to take matters into our own hands and I hit the contact on my phone that immediately connects me with Chase.

Chapter 33

Jenny

HE'S WATCHING ME WARILY FROM THE OTHER SIDE OF THE table. The breakfast that Celia has prepared has gone cold on my plate. "You need to eat something," Brian says.

The day has finally arrived and I am too nervous to eat. I can't think of anything else lately. It's all the news is talking about. Why can't they find something else to gossip about? "I just don't have an appetite," I say, pushing my chair back and dumping the rest of my food in the garbage before rinsing my plate in the sink.

"Celia's staff will do that," Brian says.

"I'm not completely helpless. I can at least rinse my dish by myself," I say.

"I didn't say you were helpless, but you're a nervous wreck. Nothing you do or say, or worry about right now will change what happens in court. What I need you to do is concentrate on getting to the courthouse safely. That is your number one priority. Chase just texted and he and Kate will meet us there and Matt will be here shortly. I just got off the phone with Paulie and while he hasn't seen any suspicious movements, Scottie apparently hasn't been filling him in on as much lately, either."

"You think Scottie knows that you and Paulie suspect him?" I ask.

"It's a pretty good possibility, but I can't dwell on it. Paulie knows how to handle himself and will get out of the situation if he thinks there's danger. You have everything you need? Our ride will be here shortly," he says.

"Yeah, I just need to brush my teeth and hair and I'll be ready to go," I say, running up the stairs just to get rid of some pent-up energy. I glance down at my phone as I brush my hair out and smile at Kate's note.

Message: Chase and I will be at the courthouse today. Love you!

Reply: Can't wait to see you!! Love you, too.

Message: Are you leaving shortly?

Reply: As we text! Brian's being so overprotective! How we're getting there is a "big secret."

Message: When is he not that way about you?? I heard Chase and Brian talking but in the dark here, too.

Message: Men!

Reply: They are a bit on the controlling side. LOL

Message: OMG, totally. Better sign off he's ready to go.

Reply: See you later.

"You ready?" Brian asks, kissing my lips.

"I'm ready."

"Good, let's go through a few things. Matt and Keith have the security teams in place. We'll take the limo to a private strip not far from here and transfer to the plane. They've got another limo that will head to LAX and a plane that will be used as a decoy just in case we're being watched. The first limo has already left, and we're safe to take off," he says, walking me out the door with him.

"Morning, Jenny," Matt says as I get into the back seat of the limo and Keith closes the door behind us.

"Morning."

"How are you holding up?" he asks.

"I've been better, but I can't change anything that's about to happen so I just need to get through it," I say.

Brian pulls me close. "Good girl, let us do all the worrying," he says.

We get on the plane and I look around. "This is much different than your other Gulfstream, Brian," I say, recalling the over-the-top decorations of his other jet. This interior is lined with sleek black leather couches that extend in a curved manner outward from both ends into ottomans. There is a marble bar at the end of one, and overhead black television monitors and a small dining area for two adjacent to the window.

"It's absolutely gorgeous and so different than the other one with the entire black and white décor," I say, looking around.

"I need variety in all things," he says, mischievously.

"I think you had enough variety last night," I say.

"I'll be the judge of that," he says, scooping me up and taking me into the bedroom with him. "Right now, I think a little stress relief is in order and we have hours to play, little one," he says.

When we're done I lay breathless in his arms. The only things keeping me together are his arms and his heartbeat. The thought of my mom left on her own to raise the kids and put up with my brother's shit is just too much and now more than that, the feeling of never being in Brian's arms again. I will myself not to cry, to be strong, and not to worry about something I have no control over.

"Sweetheart, your worry is hampering your breathing. Breathe deep, inhale, and now release," he instructs and I do.

"Again," he demands, kissing me on the forehead. "Good girl, again," he says, breathing with me.

"Deep, in and out, keep breathing," he says, reaching into the nightstand and pulling out a set of what look like silver and diamond bracelets. I look at him in surprise and his crystalline blue eyes are serious and penetrating.

"We've had restrained sex before, but I know this is different. They were just soft ties and suede cuffs. I want you to trust me and let me bind you," he says calmly, reaching for my wrists.

He turns my hands over, kissing my palm gently and I allow him to place the silver cuff over my right wrist, leaving it open before moving to the next wrist and applying the other. "There, trust me Sweetheart," he says, closing the locks. They tighten slightly around my wrists and I feel a moment of panic. "Focus on me, on my eyes, on your breathing Jenny," he says, allowing me to adjust to their feeling on my wrists without locking or affixing them to anything. "Now your ankle," he says and I let him slip the bracelet cuff with a silver and diamond lock around my ankle. He leaves it unlocked while placing me in the other. "Beautiful, now lay back for me and let me close them. I won't affix them to anything," he says.

I do as he asks inhaling deeply and as I begin to shut my eyes he slowly closes the locks on both cuffs. "Eyes on me, Jenny," he says.

"Now I want you to lay very still, legs apart, and wrists over your head, completely bound for me," he says, kissing each of my toes and running his tongue along my instep. The feeling goes straight to my groin and I moan. "Mmm, feel me all over you Sweetheart," he says, kissing up my calves and inner thighs, gently caressing before starting again until he finally gets close to my mound and begins teasing.

I moan softly as he allows his tongue to caress my clit. "I love it when you purr for me," he says, bathing me with his caresses. I writhe with pleasure, and he makes me come time and time again before releasing my wrists and my left ankle bracelet.

"This one shall remain. I want you bound to me at all times, Sweetheart. Wherever you go, whatever you're doing you'll always feel me, knowing that I alone hold the key to unlock you from whatever it is that you're going through," he says, kissing me deeply.

<hr />

It is with care that we make our way across the city from the airport. "Jenny, when we get closer I want you to lie in Brian's lap," Matt says.

"Thank you, Matt," Brian says, smirking at my rising blush.

"We have a decoy set, but just in case I want you out of sight," Matt says from the front seat, but suddenly stops smiling. "Get down now Jenny," he yells.

"Keith, they just hit the limo," he says and I feel Brian's hand tighten on the back of my neck keeping me pushed into his lap.

"Stay down Sweetheart," Brian says, rubbing the back of my neck, applying pressure.

"Keep calm everyone. The plan is working. The police have them on the run. Keith, we've gotta window of time, let's get her into the courthouse," Matt says.

As the limo pulls up to the courthouse the news reporters are swarming and Brian pulls me out of his lap. "Just keep your head down and stay next to me," he says.

"Give us a few minutes to clear the area," Matt says and Brian holds me close.

Keith stops the car and opens the door, while the other security guards create a barrier around us as we walk into the courtroom. I look around and my heart stops. Ty's mom, a well-distinguished attorney in her own right is in the center of the courtroom and she doesn't take her eyes off of me as I walk in. I've only met her twice, but each time I knew the love she felt for her son and her desire for us to marry and provide her with grandchildren. I can't help the heartache she must be feeling thinking that I took her son's life away from her. I look in her direction hoping to convey that I couldn't possibly have done what she thinks I did, but she immediately looks away, focusing on her attorney.

Larry is already seated in the front of the courtroom and Brian escorts me next to him. "Breathe, Sweetheart, I'll be right behind you," he says, settling me in before taking a seat in the long pew behind me.

I barely have time to shake hands with Larry before the court announces, "All rise. Court is now in session." I am standing alongside Larry and everyone else in the courtroom and expect to be told to take a seat momentarily.

"Your Honor, new information has come to light. Unfortunately, it was sent to our attention in the night with no time to share it until now," I hear my attorney saying.

"Objection," the prosecution declares from across the room.

"Sustained," the judge says, bringing his gavel down hard. We'll call a few minute recess. Attorneys I'd like you in my chambers now, please."

"Stay here, and take a seat," Larry says before walking with the prosecutor into the room that the judge has entered. It feels like hours instead of just twenty minutes before they return.

"All rise," the bailiff says as the judge and attorneys come into the court and the judge calls the room to order.

"Based on newly found evidence the court has asked that both attorneys review the findings and develop a plan. If needed, I will allow a forty-eight-hour recess to ensure the attorneys have enough time to evaluate the newly brought forward information. Each attorney will be provided with an opportunity to accept that or ...."

"Your Honor, the offer is most gracious, but based on the information provided to the court this morning, unknown to the prosecution before said time, the prosecution rests."

Larry stands beside me. "I appreciate the court's willingness to review the information provided on such late notice and concur with the prosecution that all charges in this case should be dismissed.

The gavel comes down hard and it echoes in the courtroom. "The court rules that all charges against Jennifer Ann Torzial are hereby dismissed," the judge says.

Brian scoops me into his arms and swings me around. "You're free, Sweetheart," he says.

"Brian, what happened?" I ask breathlessly.

I HOPE you are loving Brian and Jenny can't wait to find out exactly how it happened, and what happens next in this deliciously sinful love story. Read the final exciting novel of this trilogy. Download Claimed to keep reading!!

IF YOU WANT to stay updated on the latest releases and claim a copy of an exclusive story, sign up for her newsletter

Thank you

Thank you for reading Bound, the second in the completed Merciless Tycoon trilogy. Reviews help other readers connect to books they may love. Would you be willing to help your fellow readers learn what you love about Brian and Jenny? If so, please leave a review

Acknowledgments

Wayne, my husband, thank you for always believing in me, supporting my passions, and helping me make what seemed like an impossible dream come true.

My parents and family have been a steady reminder that you can achieve your goals with determination, hard work, and commitment. Thank you!

Karla, my dear friend, who read the first book first and encouraged me to keep going, and who recommended getting other beta readers, because "You can only read a book for the first time once." Thank you for your unconditional support through all the insanity!

A special thank you to all the people who diligently bring all the aspects of these novels together and share them across the globe. It takes an army, and I may be a bit biased, but this team is fantastic!

Via's House of Vixens, is a "private" Facebook group for readers and fans to connect. If you would like to be part of this group, request to join for loads of fun!

I hope you continue reading Jenny and Brian's story in Claimed the third and final in the Merciless Tycoon's series.

About Via Mari

Contemporary romantic suspense author Via Mari likes to keep her readers on the edge, fanning themselves as the action unfolds and the heat rises. Her books, featuring the most handsome, intense males, exemplify extreme romance, with powerful men who will stop at nothing to protect the women they love.

Via was raised in both the United States and United Kingdom. Since childhood, she has enjoyed reading books that carry you away. In fact, you can still find her in the early hours of the morning, curled up in an overstuffed chair by a crackling wood fire, reading a page-turning novel, especially during the harsh winters of the Midwestern United States.

When not writing, Via spends her days with her husband. She enjoys gardening, shopping at the local farmers market, and walking in town or around a big city. And she loves traveling to research her next novel.

She also loves interacting with her readers, so feel free to connect with her on the following social media sites! If you want to stay updated on the latest releases and claim a copy of an exclusive story, sign up for her newsletter.

Made in the USA
Monee, IL
08 May 2025

17104017R00134